Her scream echoed through the woods.

I screamed his name, a sound that echoed eerily in the smoky, soggy woods. Impulsively, as Eli disappeared from sight, I lunged forward, my arms reaching out in a desperate attempt to pull him back to safety.

And in the next second, although I had heard no sound behind me, heard no rustling of leaves or footsteps on the path, hadn't once had the creepy feeling of being watched, there was suddenly rough hands on my shoulder, pushing, pushing hard.

Terrifying thrillers by Diane Hoh:

Funhouse
The Accident
The Invitation
The Train
The Fever

NIGHTMARE HALL

Student Body

DIANE HOH

SCHOLASTIC INC.
New York Toronto London Auckland Sydney

No part of this publication may be reproduced in whole or in part, or stored in a retrieval system, or transmitted in any form or by any means, electronic, mechanical, photocopying, recording, or otherwise, without written permission of the publisher. For information regarding permission, write to Scholastic Inc., 555 Broadway, New York, NY 10012.

ISBN 0-590-20299-5

12 11 10 9 8 7 6 5 4 3 2 1   5 6 7 8 9/9 0/0

Printed in the U.S.A.   01

First Scholastic printing, March 1995

Prologue

We were all so very sorry.

If only we could have changed what happened. In a second, in a minute, in a heartbeat, we'd go back to that blustery night in late March and correct our horrible mistake. Then everything would be the way it was before.

Before the fire.

Because afterward, nothing would ever be the same again.

All it takes is one careless accident that sets the wheels in motion. In one fleeting moment everything is changed. Forever. And you don't even know it's happening. You're laughing and talking and goofing around, and you don't even realize until it's too late.

When you *do* see what's happened, you wish and you hope and you pray to go back, just for that one moment, to do something differently, to erase the horror that came after. You actually kid yourself that it might be possible. But, of course, it isn't.

We thought we could learn to live with our mistake.

How could we know that someone didn't want us living with it?

How could we know that someone didn't want us *living* at all?

Being sorry wasn't enough.

Someone wanted more, much more.

Someone wanted us *dead*.

Chapter 1

It was Bay's idea to celebrate Salem University's hard-won battle against State in the semifinals by going to the state park not far from campus. That's *my* Bayard Shaw, tall, with short, butterscotch-colored hair, friendly blue eyes, and a lazy smile. Bay Shaw liked golden retrievers, seedless grapes, water sports, getting elected to things, and me, Victory Austin Alexander. That's Victory, not Victoria, although teachers have been changing it for me my whole life, thinking, apparently, that I wasn't capable of spelling my own name correctly. When I met Bay, early in our first semester at Salem and told him my name (because he *asked*), he laughed.

I was used to that. And now that I was a college freshman, I'd decided to tell the truth about where my name came from. "My parents tried for twelve years to have a child. I'm their success story. Born, at long last, in Austin, Texas. Thus the name. I'm just glad they settled on Victory rather than Triumph or Hallelujah. Or worse."

Bay was a powerhouse on campus. He was very big in student government, unusual for a first-year student, and so popular, you only had to say his name and everyone knew who you meant. And that wasn't because he was the only student named "Bay" on campus. It was because he was very good at meeting people, getting to know them, and making sure they knew him. Bay was headed for politics after graduation, and campus was his training ground.

People listened when Bayard Shaw talked.

I, on the other hand, was a lot less noticeable. Not very tall, for one thing, and I talked too quietly, or so my mother said. "You'd better learn to speak up, Tory," she had said at least a thousand times, "or no one will notice you."

My response to that was always, "Thanks for sharing that, Mom." But I knew she was right. I wasn't beautiful, like Mindy Loomis, a cheerleader and Hoop Sinclair's steady date. Mindy had skin as smooth as silk, and perfect

4

blonde hair. I'd heard it said that Mindy had the brains of a beach umbrella, but that's not true. It's just that Mindy's mother, one of those genteel southern ladies with tons of hair and perfectly applied makeup, taught Mindy never to argue with people because then they wouldn't like her. So everyone thought Mindy had no opinions about anything. Not true. She just kept them to herself. Anyway, she cried at sad movies, so I liked her.

And I'd never been the life of the party like Hoop, who attended every party held on campus even if it was on a weeknight when Coach wanted him in bed early. Hoop came to class most mornings with bags the size of small mountains under his eyes. For someone who was supposed to be a top athlete, he wasn't taking very good care of himself. I kept expecting Coach to throw him off the team, but it didn't happen. Hoop Sinclair was too valuable.

I wasn't tall, which would have got me attention, or model-thin like Natasha Moody, my roommate and best friend on campus. Nat's waist was so small, she could belt her jeans and skirts with a rubber band. Nat would never do that, of course, because she was a fashion plate who put more thought into her accessories than many generals put into planning the most strategic battle of the war.

So I wasn't beautiful and I wasn't the life of the party, and I wasn't tall and skinny. I also didn't have Eli Segal's brains or creativity. Before we left campus for Christmas break, Eli, someone I'd always thought of as shy and quiet, dressed the statue of Salem's founder that stands in the middle of the Commons in a Santa suit. The administration was not amused.

But I was. And I viewed Eli with new respect after that.

What my mother never understood when she was nagging me about "speaking up" was, I didn't *need* a whole lot of attention. Not like Bay, and Mindy, and Hoop. And even Nat, otherwise why would she take such pains with her clothing and hair and makeup? Eli, too, or he wouldn't have gone into the town of Twin Falls and rented that Santa suit. So, I guess, out of our group, I needed the least attention of all.

Which made it really hard for me when the media latched onto our story like leeches in a swamp. None of us liked it. That's not the kind of attention anyone wants. But I hated it most of all. And there was nothing I could do about it.

I remember wishing a thousand times that I were stupid, so that I could have honestly said, when asked about that night in the park, "I didn't know any better." But just as I knew I wasn't beautiful or terribly creative or charming or noticeable, I also knew I wasn't stupid. So I had no excuse for my part in what happened.

What we were celebrating that night in March was our school's triumph over State University in the basketball semifinals. We'd be going on to the finals, thanks in part to Hoop's genius on the court. He was still beaming when he met us outside the gym, and his wide, square face was still flushed, his thick blond hair damp from his shower and curling around his jumbo-sized ears.

When Bay said, "I think we should grab some hot dogs and head for the state park to celebrate," it was Eli who said, "No cooking at the park tonight, the wind's too high. No burning allowed. There are posters all over campus."

I wish it had been me, Tory Alexander, who had said that. I'd love to claim that it was, sort of let myself off the hook a little, but I'd be lying. It was Eli. *Only* Eli, although all of us had seen the posters around campus warning us, in big, black letters, of the fire hazard in the area.

Then I was glad I hadn't said it, because Bay's eyebrows disappeared into his hairline and he said in that deceptively friendly voice that I'd heard before when he was annoyed with someone, "Appreciate the input, Segal. But all we're going to do is fricassee a few hot dogs. How dangerous can that be? I've been doing it for years. Haven't set a forest on fire once."

I myself would have preferred to go into town and do some dancing at Johnny's or gone to Vinnie's for pizza. Half the school would be at Vinnie's.

So why didn't I say so? Well, for one thing, I didn't want Bay looking at me the way he was looking at Eli, and for another, I knew I was no match for Bay. He had this amazing talent for persuading people not only to do what he wanted, but to convince them that it was what *they* wanted, too. I was smart enough to see that, but not smart enough to figure out whether it was charm or manipulation. Whatever it was, it worked, and I was convinced that Bay would make a great politician some day.

If Bay wanted to go to the park and cook hot

dogs, that was what we'd do. We all knew that.

So we were surprised when Eli didn't give in right away. Eli was quiet, like me. I'd heard him argue before, but always about abstract things, like philosophy and psychology and politics. He could get very passionate about those things. But I'd never heard him disagree with anyone before on a personal matter.

Eli said, "We can't go to the park, Bay. It'll be cold without a campfire, and no fun. But we can't have one. The winter's been too dry and the wind has been fierce for a week. It still is. Building a fire in the park is just too risky."

He was right about the wind. My hair, which according to my mother I wear "too long for such a small face," was practically being yanked out of my scalp by the late-March, very brisk wind that Eli was talking about. Unlike Mindy's hair, which still looked as smooth and perfect as it had when she'd run out onto the court in her cheerleading uniform three hours earlier. How was that possible? Maybe she sprayed it with shellac.

"Eli," Bay said smoothly, "if you're worried about the fire getting out of hand, we'll grab a couple of big bottles of water when we get the hot dogs, okay? We'll keep an eagle eye on things and if so much as a spark gets away from us, I promise I'll hunt it down myself and douse it. Don't you trust me?"

Eli hesitated. He *did* trust Bay. We all did. Bay had great ideas and great follow-through and never messed up. "If we get caught by the park rangers, Bay," Eli pointed out, "we're doomed."

Now it was Bay's turn to hesitate. And I knew why. He'd once told me his college career was important not just educationally, but as a stepping-stone to politics. He'd said, very seriously, "If I screw up here, it won't matter all that much *now*. But ten or twenty years down the road, when I run for public office, anything I did that I shouldn't have will hit the papers, explode on television, and could blow me right out of the water."

Getting arrested for lighting a campfire when there was a burning ban would look bad on his record. And Bay knew that.

But he wanted to go to the park and have a campfire more than he wanted to focus on ten or twenty years in the future. I could see it in his face. And the other thing I could see in his face was a refusal to back down now that he'd already dictated what his plans were for the celebration. "Never mind the rangers," he said, and I knew he'd made up his mind. "There are only a few of them, and the park is very, very big. Acres and acres of forest primeval. We'll just go deeper into the woods. By the time the rangers smell smoke, we'll be long gone."

Mindy and Hoop whooped with delight, while Nat complained that she wasn't dressed for the woods in her short skirt and sweater, but everyone was already headed for Bay's battered old station wagon. He called it the Bus because it was always delivering people here or there on campus. He could afford a much nicer car, but joked that he wanted everyone to know he was "just one of the common people." "Can't win friends and influence people if you're driving around in luxury while they're pedalling across campus on their bikes in the rain," he'd told me once.

I was sandwiched in between Bay and Eli in the front seat. Although Bay seemed perfectly relaxed, driving with one hand so he could hold my hand, Eli felt stiff and tense beside me. I wanted to say something to him, but couldn't think what. I thought he was right to be worried about the burning ban, but I also knew if I said that, Bay would be mad and our celebration would be ruined.

Still, during the short drive along the highway with the grocery bags on my lap and Eli's, each time a leaf or twig was flung against the windshield by the brisk wind that bent the saplings on the edge of the woods almost double, I stirred uneasily on the front seat, remembering the posters tacked all across campus.

As if he'd read my mind, Bay said suddenly, "There's never been a forest fire in the park."

Eli looked up with interest. He'd been silently studying the floorboards ever since we left the convenience store. The only conversation had been coming from the backseat where Hoop was giving Nat and Mindy a play-by-play description of the game. As Hoop continued talking, Eli leaned across me and said to Bay, "How do you know that? That there haven't been any forest fires in the park?"

"I asked. One of the rangers was tacking up a poster, and I asked him how long it had been since they'd had a fire, and he said they'd never had one. So you can quit worrying, Eli. I know that's what you're doing. I can feel it. You're going to spoil our celebration and make me wish I'd left you back on campus."

Eli tried. I could almost feel him trying. He sank back against the seat and stretched out his long legs and whistled under his breath, as if he were the most relaxed person in the world.

But a little pulse at his temple was throbbing

and the high, perfectly sculpted cheekbones in his thin, narrow face were flushed with red.

I found myself turning my head to glance at Bay, whose eyes were on the road ahead of him. It was so like Bay to insist on the park even though he'd actually talked to a ranger about the burning ban. That ranger had probably added a warning or two of his own. If that conversation had been with any of the rest of us, we would have changed our plans and gone to Johnny's or Vinnie's instead.

Why hadn't Bay? It wasn't as if he was constantly looking for risky things to do. He'd meant what he said about not screwing up in college. Was it just his unwillingness to change his plans that kept him driving toward the park?

"We could still go dancing," I said quietly over the sound of Hoop's triumphant voice from the backseat. "I mean, maybe the park's closed. Wouldn't they close it if there really was a fire hazard?"

"No," Eli said flatly before Bay could answer. "People do a lot of things in the park besides sit around a fire. They hike, they jog, they take the nature trails. Or they just hang out, because it's a great place to do that. There's no reason why the park shouldn't be used as long as everyone obeys the burning ban."

"Well, thank you for that, Smokey the Bear," Bay muttered, and expertly whipped the wheel around to take the sharp turn into the park.

We were there.

So why did I suddenly not feel like celebrating? And why did I suddenly wish fiercely that Bay had listened to Eli, turned the Bus around, and driven back to campus?

More important, why didn't I *say* something? Why didn't I insist that we go back? Maybe that one time I could have spoken up in a loud, authoritative voice and people would have listened. Maybe it would have made a difference.

Instead, I jumped out of the car with everyone else and carried my bag of groceries into the deepest part of the woods.

And I helped gather wood for the fire.

Then, for two hours we sat around the fire Bay and Hoop had built. I couldn't help noticing that while they stacked the wood, Eli had busied himself selecting CDs for the portable player Bay had brought. I had to admire Eli's stubbornness. He wasn't making an issue of his disapproval. He just wasn't participating in the building of the fire. I've wished many times since then that I'd done something, anything, to say I felt the same way.

If I had, maybe I'd feel better about what happened later.

Eli did join us around the fire though, and even said how good it felt. Late March in the northeast isn't the tropics. And then there was the wind, whipping our hair around our faces and tugging nastily at our clothes. It was chilly out there in those deep, windblown woods.

We all sat very close together and kept the fire small. True to his word, Bay chased after the tiniest of glowing embers swept up by the wind and tossed into the forest. We cooked our hot dogs, talked about the game, made s'mores with the graham crackers, marshmallows, and chocolate bars Eli had bought, and sang to the music on the portable CD player.

And after a while all of us, even Eli, forgot about the posters on campus and the threat of detection and any possible punishment. I rested my head on Bay's shoulder. Nat, wearing Eli's denim jacket to protect her expensive hand-knit sweater, lay on the mossy ground, her head propped up on a folded tarp, her eyes closed, lazily snapping her fingers in time to the music playing. Mindy and Hoop were sitting so close together that, in the shadows created by the fire, their blond heads seemed to blend into one. Eli sat off to one side, his back against a tree, his long legs stretched out in front of him. His dark hair, longer than Bay's, blew around his face, and his eyes were closed.

Content in the triumph of the game, our hunger satisfied, and lulled by the music, the red-and-orange dancing flames, and the company of good friends, we all relaxed.

That was our mistake.

Because I was leaning against Bay's chest, I couldn't tell that he, like Eli, had closed his eyes. Nat was lying on her back, staring up at the sky, Mindy and Hoop were looking only at each other, and I'd closed my eyes, too.

So no one saw the ember snatched up by the fierce wind and tossed recklessly into the woods, land in the very heart of a parched, dry pine tree. No one saw the second ember, or the third, or the fourth.

But there had to have been at least that many, because when Eli suddenly cried out and we all looked to see why he'd yelled, we saw fire consuming not just the tall, skinny pine tree to our right, but two more blazes taking hold of a tree directly in front of us and swallowing up a crackling bush to our left.

"The water!" Bay shouted, jumping to his feet, "grab the water bottles!"

As if the bottled water could possibly douse the fire in that tall pine tree, already roaring with flames so high above our heads. We needed a faucet, and we needed a long hose, and we knew it.

But we tried, anyway. The water was in gallon jugs. We ripped the caps off and splashed it wildly, one bottle after another. Nat and I tackled the large bush, while Hoop and Eli tried desperately to swing their jugs upward, high enough to dampen the pine tree ahead of us. Bay did the same with the pine tree to our left.

It was hopeless. Even as, screaming crazily, we raced about with our pitifully ineffective jugs, the flames in the pine tree jumped like scampering squirrels to the tree beside it, which immediately exploded into an inferno. Flames lit up the sky.

Embers from the bush had already leaped sideways into a larger bush beside it, and Nat and I were out of water. The jugs were empty.

The wind didn't help. It roared around us, whipping the flames into a frenzy, yanking them from treetop to treetop, from bush to bush, darting every few minutes or so back down to our fire to scoop up even more red-hot embers and toss them into the woods.

When the sky above us was red with fire and the heat was becoming intense, Bay ran back to Nat and me, waving his empty jug and shouting, "We've got to get out of here!" He gestured toward the ring of bushes beside us, completely engulfed in flames now and the pine trees in front of us, roaring a protest as the fire swallowed them up. "If we don't leave now, we'll be trapped in here. Don't leave your jugs behind! Don't leave *anything* behind. There can't be any sign that we were here! Hurry up!"

Later, it would strike me how amazing it was that even as we stood there, sweating and panic-stricken, our very lives threatened, Bay had the presence of mind to think about the peril of leaving evidence behind. This, I told myself when I did think of it, is why everyone trusts Bay. Because he thinks of everything.

And later still, I would change my mind. I would think that if we hadn't trusted Bay in the first place, none of it would have happened. But that was unfair. We all went to the park. We all watched and helped as the campfire was built. And we all relaxed after a while and closed our eyes.

When no one moved in response to Bay's

order, he shouted, "We can't be found here! Even if we're not killed, they'll know we did it! We've got to get out of here right *now!*"

Snapping out of our shock and fear, we grabbed our stuff and ran.

Chapter 2

I remember only two things about that race through the woods. I remember the sound of the flames exploding above us as they leaped from treetop to treetop, and I remember trying desperately to keep my footing as I ran. The ground was dry, but covered with pine needles and every bit as slippery as mud. Nat, running ahead of me, was wearing smooth-soled flats, and having a terrible time remaining upright. She kept clutching at tree limbs and bushes to maintain her balance, and that was slowing her down. Eli, seeing her struggle, raced past me and grabbed her elbow to propel her along the path.

I don't remember anything else. Sometimes I think of it as a movie I'm watching: six good friends who, only minutes before, had been having a wonderful time, now tearing through the dense, dark woods, their only light the orange-red glow of the flames racing to catch up with them. Someone is sobbing . . . the tall, thin girl wearing a short skirt and sweater so unsuitable for running through the woods? Someone else is shouting in a deep, authoritative voice. It's the tall, good-looking boy, telling everyone to "hurry up, hurry up, I think I hear sirens already. If they catch us . . ." That boy's the hero, I think as I watch my movie. He sounds like one. Looks like one, too, and he's giving the orders.

So who is the heroine, I wonder. There's always a heroine. I know it's not the small girl in jeans and a red sweater and sneakers, the girl with long, dark hair flying around her terrified face, because I know that's me, and I'm *not* a heroine. And I don't think it's the girl who's slipping and sliding all over the place, because she's wearing the wrong kind of shoes for a needle-strewn path in the woods. A heroine wouldn't be wearing the wrong kind of shoes.

Maybe it's the beautiful girl with hair that is smooth in spite of the horrendous wind and the heat and the frantic dash along the rough, winding path. A true movie heroine wouldn't let her hair get messed up, so maybe it's her.

But she's crying. Not crying in an attractive, tears-sliding-gently-down-the-cheeks crying, Hollywood-style, but crying in huge, loud gulps. Her mouth is open and her nose is running. So maybe she's not the heroine. Maybe there isn't one in this movie.

They race along the path, the small group trying to escape the terrible roar of the flames chasing them. They stumble a lot on the uneven surface, and the girl in the sweater and skirt would have fallen repeatedly if the tall, thin boy with long, dark brown hair wasn't gripping her elbow so tightly. His lips are clamped together tightly, his gray eyes grim, but he doesn't let go of her elbow.

The faster they run, the faster the flames seem to leap from tree to tree, the dry branches exploding instantly. The sound seems to be coming closer and closer to the runners.

And now another sound, the shrill scream of sirens, is louder.

The boy who might be the hero because he shouts with such authority, curses at the sirens and commands again. "Hurry up! We've got to get out of here before those fire trucks arrive."

I watch the movie playing out in my mind, see the flames spreading in a semicircle directly behind the cast, and know that they're not going to make it. No way are they going to outrun those leaping, racing flames about to engulf them.

But we did.

Thanks to Bay urging us on, never letting us stop for a second to take a breath. We got to the car while the sirens were still a safe distance away.

"We can't go back the way we came," Bay said grimly as we all threw ourselves into the Bus. Nat and Mindy, exhausted, tumbled in over the open tailgate, lying, gasping, on the platform created by the small third seat being down. We had put the seat down to create a level space for our cooler full of drinks, which Bay had snatched up before we raced away from the fire. The cooler had his name on the inside of the lid. "Evidence," he would have called it.

Eli and I slid into the front seat. He was breathing so heavily, I was afraid he was going to pass out.

"If we go back to school the way we came, we'll run into those sirens," Bay continued. "Fire trucks, maybe, but the cops could be right behind them. They'll see us. We'll have to go the long way around."

None of us said anything. We couldn't speak.

We were so out of breath that it would be long minutes before any of us could say a word. It didn't matter, because we wouldn't have known what to say, anyway. We were all in shock. The knowledge of what we'd done hadn't sunk in yet. We weren't acting out of thought, we were acting out of instinct.

Awareness would come later, and with it, pain and regret and horror like none of us had ever known before.

Bay threw the car into reverse, whipped the wheel around, and raced out of the parking lot. I turned my head just once. My stomach rolled over when I saw nothing behind us but a thick wall of flames gobbling up the park. The woods seemed to be bathed in orange light.

In the backseat, Mindy wailed, "What are we going to do? What are we going to do? They're going to find out we did it, and we're all going to go to jail!"

"It wasn't our fault," Bay said in a strained voice I didn't recognize. "It was the wind."

"Which," Eli reminded him, "is exactly why the rangers imposed a burning ban."

"If you say 'I told you so,' " Bay said from between clenched teeth, "I'll stop the car right now and push you out myself."

"Sorry," Eli said. "I guess we should just be grateful we all got out alive."

And that was when Natasha pulled herself to a sitting position. That was when she looked into the backseat. That was when she said in an odd, anxious voice, "Where's Hoop?"

The three of us in the front seat swivelled.

Hoop was not sitting in the backseat.

But he should have been. He was *supposed* to be there, gasping for breath like the rest of us, sweaty and scared, his hair windblown.

Only he wasn't. The backseat was empty. The rest of us stared, refusing to believe the horrible fact that was beginning to dawn on us.

One of us was missing.

One of us hadn't made it out of the fire.

Chapter 3

Bay stared at the empty backseat for so long, the car veered off the road onto the shoulder, scattering pebbles everywhere. He cursed, whipped his head to the front, and clutched the wheel tightly as he wrestled the Bus back onto the highway.

But Eli and I were still staring at the backseat, where there was no Hoop.

"Nat, he's not back there with you?" I asked. My voice sounded tinny, as if it were whining through a bad telephone connection.

"No, he's not."

"Mindy, you were with him," Eli said. His voice sounded as weird as mine. "You were running along the path with him. Didn't he stay with you? Where *is* he?" Before Nat could answer, Eli said, "Bay, stop the car! Stop it, now!"

Bay screeched to a halt on the highway.

"Mindy?" the three of us said in one voice.

"I don't *know* where he is!" she wailed. "I was so scared! He was behind me in the beginning, and I just thought he was still behind me. I was too scared to turn around and look."

No one said anything. We sat in the car in a stunned, sick silence while the sirens nearing the park grew louder.

"Bay," Eli said calmly, his voice normal now, "turn the car around. We have to go back."

"Sure, sure we do," Bay agreed hurriedly, nodding. "Hoop must have fallen. That path was slippery. But," he peered out the windshield, "there isn't enough room here to turn around. I'll have to go on up ahead, look for a side road."

Eli sat up very straight, one hand on the dashboard. "There's no time for that," he protested. "If Hoop fell and he's in the middle of that fire . . . . Come on, Bay, just back up onto the shoulder and turn around. It's okay, there's no traffic coming. We can't waste time looking for a turnaround now. We've got to get back to the park."

Still Bay didn't back up. He just sat there, the engine running, his foot on the brake. I knew he was probably biting on his lower lip, something he always does when he's concentrating.

It was Mindy who said what everyone wanted to hear. "Hoop can take care of himself." She sat up. Her voice was low, almost a whisper, but composed. She sounded like an authority on Hoop, which, of course, she was. "He's a super athlete, remember? I don't know how he got separated from us, but he'll be okay on his own. Really. He *will*."

When no one argued with her, because we wanted to believe what she was saying, her voice gained strength. "Hoop wouldn't want us to go back there. He wouldn't want us to risk everything, risk getting thrown out of school, maybe even tossed into jail, when he can take perfectly good care of himself. He's probably already back at the frat house, waiting for us. He spends a lot of time running in those woods and knows a lot of shortcuts back to school. He must have found one."

"If he'd found a shortcut," Eli said evenly, "he would have taken us with him."

"What probably happened," Mindy persisted, "is that Hoop got separated from us by the smoke and the flames, and by the time he found one of the shortcuts, we were too far ahead of him. And now that I think about it, I'm pretty sure I *did* hear someone yelling behind us. But we were all making so much noise, I didn't realize it was Hoop. If we'd paid attention and gone with him, we'd all be back on campus by now, too."

I could *feel* Eli wrestling with Mindy's theory. He wanted to believe her, as we all did.

Eli didn't have any family. He was the only one of us who had no one. He was struggling to put himself through school with the help of scholarships and summer jobs and a part-time job in the cafeteria at Devereaux where Nat and I roomed. That's where I'd met him, and then he had introduced me to Bay and the others.

We all knew how important college was to Eli. With his brilliant mind, it would be positively obscene for him to miss out on a college education.

And everything he'd worked so hard and so long for would go straight down the toilet if we went looking for Hoop and got caught in the park now.

"You really think he found a shortcut?" he asked Mindy, a trace of hope in his voice.

"Yes," she said, tentatively at first, then she

repeated it with more emphasis. "Yes. I'm sure he did. If he hadn't, he'd be in the car right now, wouldn't he?"

We were all thinking, *Unless something happened to him*. I waited for someone to say it, but no one did.

It wasn't only Bay and Eli who had a lot to lose if we got caught. Mindy had been groomed by her mother since she was two years old to win every beauty pageant that existed. She'd already won several. Some people think that's silly, but there *are* girls and mothers like that out there, or the pageants would have died out a long time ago. Mindy's mother had been Miss Cotton Ball or something like that a million years ago. She was determined that Mindy would not only follow in her footsteps, but end up taking the biggest crown there was, maybe Miss Planet or Miss Deep Space Nine or something. Dance lessons, singing lessons, baton lessons, Miss Totter's School of Etiquette for Young Ladies, that had been Mindy's life when she was growing up. It sounded repulsive to me, but Mindy was used to it. And by now, almost as determined as her mother to take home a houseful of sparkling crowns.

Someone who had been expelled from college for starting a forest fire didn't stand a chance of being elected dogcatcher, much less picked to represent the entire planet as an example of fine, upstanding Young Womanhood.

Still, Mindy *was* in love with Hoop. So I figured she really must have been convinced he was safe, or she'd insist that we go back.

As for Nat, what college meant to her was a chance to become a doctor. Her younger sister, Dorie, had juvenile diabetes. Nat had made up her mind years before to study medicine and help her sister. Of all of us, only Nat was more determined than Bay to succeed in college and go on to the goal she'd had in mind since she was ten.

Me, I had my own reasons for not wanting to go back. My family had moved from Texas to Rochester, New York, when I was in high school, and I'd been scared to death of attending a huge new school. I was also absolutely certain that I was the ugliest, dullest, fifteen-year-old to ever grace the continent. Why would anyone attractive or popular or smart want to be my friend? So, I sought out in my new school the most unsavory, unattractive, unpopular group I could find.

I won't go into the grubby details, except to say that I narrowly escaped being thrown out of school on several occasions, narrowly escaped being tossed out of my own house by my exasperated, disappointed parents, and very narrowly escaped ruining my entire life.

What turned me around was a car wreck involving four of my friends. Drinking was involved. I wasn't in the car at the time, because I'd been grounded for the nine-millionth time that year. But one of my friends died.

It was a very sobering, scary experience.

I got my act together, and applied to Salem University in upstate New York. The day I was accepted I felt I'd been given a fresh start.

I loved Salem, loved its beautiful, rolling green lawns, its tall, red brick buildings, loved the sprawling green Commons where on nice days we all lay on blankets studying, talking, joking around. I even liked all of my classes. I was grateful every single day that I hadn't thrown away my life.

Being caught near the park now would do that, though. I'd be right back where I was in high school, only this time I didn't think my parents would be so forgiving. They were thrilled and relieved by my "adjustment" to college, ecstatic about my grades, and liked my new friends, whom they'd met on Parents' Day.

I couldn't imagine calling my folks to say I'd

been thrown out of school, or that I was in jail. They had probably anticipated a phone call like that once upon a time, but not now. Their hopes for me were up again, and if I blew those hopes out of the water, I didn't see how they could ever forgive me.

We all had our reasons for not wanting to return to the park.

So we listened to Mindy and let her convince us. We told ourselves that after all, Mindy *loved* Hoop and would be the last person in the world to abandon him if she thought he wasn't safe.

We sat there on the highway in Bay's old car, hearing the sirens closing in on the park entrance, telling ourselves that our friend, Hoop Sinclair, was already safely back on campus.

"I think," Nat said then, "that we should just find a phone and call the frat house and make sure that Hoop is there, safe and sound, okay? There's probably a phone right up ahead, so if he isn't at the Sigma house we can turn right around and go back to look for him."

We all agreed that her idea made sense. Why turn around and risk running into the police when a simple phone call would tell us what we needed to know? There would be a phone just up ahead, so what kind of time were we talking about? Only a minute or two.

It was actually five minutes or more before we spotted a highway telephone. By that time one of us, I don't remember who, pointed out that we were so close to campus now, we might just as well take another minute or two to go the rest of the way and check at the Sigma house in person. Each of us had called there at one time or another, and the house was so chaotic, so unorganized, that it often took many minutes for someone to locate Hoop and send him to the phone. We didn't want to waste all that time, we told each other.

So we drove on.

When we got to the frat house, we found a really raucous party going on in celebration of Salem's basketball triumph earlier that night. People were clustered on the lawn in front of the big, columned, white house, lights blazed inside, and music blared through the open front door.

Mindy looked out the back window of the station wagon and said in a shaky voice, "I'll never find him in all that mess. Maybe I should just go straight back to the sorority house and call from there."

It was clear to all of us that she was suddenly afraid of what she'd learn if she went to the door and asked for Hoop. We were, too.

It was Eli who drew the line. "You are *going* up there, Mindy," he said evenly, "and you are going to find out if Hoop is inside."

While she was gone, we all held our breath.

She was back a few minutes later, and she was smiling. "He's there," she cried triumphantly as she climbed back into the car. "I told you he would be. Wow, we came so close to blowing everything, and all the time he was right here, safe. I could strangle him, though, for worrying us like that."

Eli swivelled around to face her. "You saw Hoop? Talked to him?"

"Well, no, I didn't. I didn't actually *see* him. It was a madhouse in there. But I talked to Boomer, and he said he was sure he'd seen Hoop just a few minutes ago. And just to be sure, I checked with some other guys and they all said of course Hoop was there, why wouldn't he be?"

Although Eli shook his head, the rest of us agreed that Boomer, a football player we all liked and trusted, would never have said that Hoop was there if he wasn't. Then someone, Nat, I think, said she was really exhausted and could Bay please take us back to the dorm now, and Bay said that if Eli was still worried, he could always call the frat house and talk to Hoop himself, when he got back to his dorm.

We drove away from Sigma house.

I wondered, as we pulled away from the curb, what we would have done if Hoop *hadn't* been there. We couldn't have gone back to the park by then. Because the sirens had stopped. That meant the fire trucks and the police and heaven only knew who else . . . reporters? were already at the park.

So *we* certainly couldn't be.

We *couldn't*. Might as well just drive into town, walk into the police station, find a cell, step inside, and swing the door shut.

Besides, Hoop was okay.

He was in the frat house, just as Mindy had said he would be.

Chapter 4

You'd have thought that we'd have been jabbering like crazy with relief as we drove away from the frat house.

But no one said a word. Because even with Hoop safe at the Sigma house, there was still the fire. We could see it now, off in the distance, turning the late night sky into a bizarre orange sunset.

I wondered how long it would take the Sigma party-goers on the lawn to notice, and what they would think when they did. If they guessed that it was a fire, they'd pile into their cars and race to the scene, creating a mess on the highway as they rubbernecked.

Why was I even thinking of that now? I had other problems.

To cover up the awkward, painful silence, Bay switched on the car radio. But instead of music, which would have helped, we heard an announcer's voice saying, "*Repeat, this is a bulletin, just in. We have received word that a major fire is raging at this moment at the state park, in the area just west of Salem University. All citizens are being warned away from that area, and roadblocks are being set up by the state police. No casualties have been reported at this time, and word from the fire marshal is that none are expected, as the park was believed empty of visitors at the time the fire began. We will provide additional details on this late-breaking story as we receive them.*"

No one commented on the news story, and our miserable silence deepened.

I was never so glad to get out of a car in my life. None of us even said good night or our usual "see you tomorrow" or mentioned any weekend plans.

All I wanted, personally, was to get away from everyone, all of them, as fast as possible. I figured they probably felt pretty much the same way. I wanted the night to be over. I wanted to go to bed and to sleep and wake up on Saturday morning believing that none of it had happened. We hadn't gone to the park, hadn't built a campfire, the embers hadn't been tossed into the woods by the wind, and the state park was as peaceful and pretty as it had ever been.

But I knew it wasn't going to be like that when I awoke on Saturday morning. No nightmare, this. All of it was real.

If only we'd gone dancing at Johnny's instead, or to the Sigma party, or to Vinnie's for pizza. If only we hadn't cooked hot dogs. If only, if only, if only . . .

I'd said the same thing when my friends in high school drove their car into a freight train. I'd said, If only they hadn't been drinking, if only they hadn't taken *that* road, if only I'd been with them, maybe I'd have made them take a different road, one without a railroad crossing. If only, if only, if only . . . and now, years later, here I was, thinking the same thing again.

I felt stupid. Hadn't I learned anything at all since then?

When we got to our room and threw ourselves down on our beds, Nat switched on the radio, the dial set, as it always was, to the campus radio station.

Before I could yell, "Please don't do that! They'll just be talking about the fire and I don't want to hear it," the voice of Ian Banion, a friend of ours, began speaking. His deep, authoritative voice resonated in our room with a blood-curdling statement.

"This just in. Although rangers fighting the blaze at the state park west of campus had initially believed the area to be free of visitors when the fire began, we have just received word that a body has been discovered at the scene."

Nat and I bolted upright at the same moment.

"Fire Marshal Edmund Cervantes is unwilling to speculate at this point as to whether or not the victim might be a student at this university. Our reporter was informed that Cervantes was on his way to the scene and would notify the administration if warranted. A reporter from this station is on the scene and will notify us as soon as the identity of the victim is known."

"No," Nat breathed, her face a sickly gray. "No!"

"The fire is now believed to be under control. Cervantes has told our reporter that it is too early to assess the damages in terms of acreage destroyed or dollar amounts. We will have more on this story in fifteen minutes. Stay tuned."

"Turn it off!" I screamed from my bed, "turn it off!"

Nat switched off the radio. Her eyes were bleak as she looked over at me. "Hoop?" she whispered. "You don't think . . . you don't think it could be Hoop, do you? I mean, Boomer said . . ."

"No," I whispered back, "it can't be Hoop. How could it be? He's at Sigma house." I shook my head vigorously. "No, no, it's not Hoop, it's *not!*"

But I had this awful, clammy feeling in my chest. And the expression on Nat's long, narrow face said that she had it, too. Because there hadn't been anyone else at that park when we got there except the six of us. We hadn't heard a sound, hadn't seen any sign of other visitors.

And Mindy hadn't actually *seen* Hoop at the Sigma house.

I had always liked Hoop a lot. Like Mindy, he was no genius, and he had a notoriously bad temper, often losing it on the basketball court, but he was good-hearted. He was the only one of us who didn't sweat college. He was attending because he hadn't wanted to quit playing basketball after high school, so when Salem offered him an athletic scholarship, he took it. He seemed fairly confident that he had a good chance at playing professional ball and since that was the only thing he wanted to do, his education so far consisted of only the easiest classes.

I wondered sometimes what he would do with his life if he didn't make it in the NBA. Mindy had this lovely fantasy of winning a string of beauty pageants, spending a year or two travelling and becoming famous, and then returning to wherever Hoop happened to be playing ball at the time, and marrying him. Of course he would be famous by then, too. They would buy a mansion, probably in South Carolina somewhere near her mother, have two-point-four beautiful, gifted children, and live a lifestyle suited to the Rich and Famous. They would be two of The Beautiful People.

But now . . .

"What should we do?" Nat whispered, clutching her comforter to her chest. "We should do something."

I couldn't think. I couldn't speak. I couldn't move. I sat on my bed feeling as if someone had just hosed me down with ice water. The thought of Hoop dying in that fire was more than I could stand. Hoop burning? His skin on fire, his honest, open face, his hair, too . . . the image made me physically ill.

I lurched from my bed and ran into the bathroom, where I threw up every last trace of our picnic in the park.

When I came back into the room, a wet washcloth in my hands, Nat was just hanging up the phone. "He's not dead!" she shouted, jumping up and down. "The fire victim isn't dead!"

I collapsed on my bed. "What?"

"That was Bay on the phone. I called him to see if he'd heard that they'd found a body, and he corrected me. Said it wasn't a body, after all. He said they just came on the radio and said that the fire victim was still alive, after all. Barely. But alive." Some of Nat's natural color had returned to her face. "You made me turn off the radio too soon, Tory. We should have kept listening."

I tried to take in what she was saying. "Have they identified the person yet?" I asked, my heart pounding crazily.

She shook her head. "No. Not yet."

"I'm going to call the Sigma house and find out if Hoop is there. I can't stand not knowing another second."

I called Sigma house.

Hoop wasn't there.

And the person I spoke with was very annoyed, because Hoop was a Sigma and he was the game's hero, and yet he hadn't even bothered to celebrate at their party. No one had seen him since the game. "Went off with some friends of his," Hoop's frat brother grumbled. "No one here knows exactly where, and he isn't back yet."

I asked to speak to Boomer, who had told Mindy he'd seen Hoop, but when he finally came on the line, he not only didn't remember ever seeing Hoop at the party, he didn't remember speaking to Mindy, either.

I sagged against the wall, the telephone still in my hand, even though Boomer had already hung up.

"He's not there, is he?" Nat demanded. "I don't believe this! How could he not be there? Where *is* he, then?" She lifted her head and stared at me, the bleak, desolate look returning to her eyes. "Tory," she said softly, "what are we going to do?"

Chapter 5

Before Nat could ask me again what we should do, there was a knock on our door.

I answered it with my heart in my throat because I expected to see a police officer standing in the hallway. I found Bay and Eli standing there instead. They looked a hundred years older than they had when we'd sat on the fountain wall on the Commons earlier that day making plans for the evening. Setting fire to the park hadn't been discussed as an option.

"He's not dead," Bay said abruptly, brushing past me and on into the room. "Did Nat tell you that guy they found in the fire isn't dead?"

Eli followed Bay into the room, took a seat on the floor beside my desk. I closed the door and went back to sit on my bed with my knees up, my arms encircling them, my head down. "Yes. Of course she told me. Then I called

Sigma house." I lifted my head to look directly at Bay. "Hoop isn't there. Hasn't *been* there. They don't know where he is."

"Oh, for pete's sake!" Eli burst out, "who are we kidding? Can we please quit tiptoeing around this and admit that it was Hoop they found?"

Nat gasped. "You don't *know* that!" she cried.

"Yes, I *do*. And so do you. We all do. Boomer was wrong about Hoop being at the party, and we all know it. Mindy probably knows it by now, too, which is why she didn't answer her phone when I called just now. She's trying to deny it. But it's there. And we can't pretend it isn't. The first thing we have to deal with," Eli added firmly, "is that he hasn't been identified. We have to let someone know his name, so his family can be notified."

"Are you really that sure it's him?" Nat asked him in a forlorn voice. "We shouldn't tell them it is if it isn't. I mean, couldn't it be a hitchhiker, or a jogger out for a run, or someone walking his dog? It could be, couldn't it?"

Eli's gray eyes were full of skepticism. "It could. But that's about as likely as it being a leprechaun who'd been hiding under a toadstool. I mean, if that isn't Hoop, then where exactly do you think he might be right about now? He's not with us. He's not at Sigma house. And he isn't with Mindy, or she'd have called us. So what do *you* think the chances are that Hoop wasn't the person found lying in those burned woods?"

Silence. After a minute or so, quiet tears began spilling down Nat's cheeks. She didn't bother to wipe them away.

"So, what do you suggest, Einstein?" Bay said, looking at Eli. "If we tell someone that's our friend Hoop lying in a hospital bed, they'll ask how we know, won't they? And what do we tell them then?"

Eli didn't answer, just shook his head and stared at the floor.

But after a minute or two, Nat said softly, "We could say he was alone in the woods."

All three of us stared at her.

She flushed, but she didn't look away. "We could say we had an argument with him and he left us to go running in the woods. Everyone knows he has a temper. And everyone knows he ran a lot in the park. We could say that when he didn't come back, we got worried, and started looking for him, and then we heard about the fire, so we thought it might be him. We could say that."

I was nodding. The important thing right then was to let someone know Hoop's identity. "Maybe that would work," I said. "That way, we could tell them who he is without admitting that we were with him. And saying that we'd had an argument would explain to Hoop's other friends why we weren't with him in the park. That's the first thing they're going to ask. They're going to say, 'Where were *you* when Hoop got trapped in that fire?'"

Bay was nodding, too, and chewing on his lower lip.

"You're forgetting something," Eli reminded us. "Hoop isn't *dead*. Probably unconscious, maybe even in a coma. It sounded pretty bad on the radio. But he's not dead. If he recovers, he'll be able to tell someone what happened. He's not going to lie about who was with him at the time the fire started. Why would he?"

"Because we'd do the same for him, and he knows it," Nat countered. "As long as he's lucid when he comes to and isn't drugged out or something. If he's thinking at all, he won't hang us out to dry. Hoop wouldn't do that. He wasn't like that."

We realized at the same time Nat did that she'd used past tense. Her face drained of all color and tears welled up again. "I mean," she stammered, "isn't. He *isn't* like that. Besides, Hoop may not be as smart as Eli, but he's not stupid. He'll realize right away that if he tells the truth, he'll be in as much trouble as we are. Good-bye scholarship, good-bye college, and most important, good-bye basketball forever, except on a playground somewhere. So in a way, we're protecting *him* as much as we are ourselves."

"What makes you think," Eli said slowly, "that if we tell that story, and the cops buy it, that they won't hang Hoop for the fire? According to you, he was in the woods alone. And there was a fire. You want him to take the blame?"

"Eli," Bay said, "you surprise me. You're supposed to be the genius here. But even I can figure out that the fire marshal must have found the remains of our campfire by now. Why would a lone runner stop to build a campfire?"

Eli thought for a minute and then said stubbornly, "He wasn't wearing jogging clothes. They're not going to think that's weird?"

"That's because he wasn't *planning* on a jog when he met us," Nat said patiently. "He only went running because he lost his temper and was furious with us. So, of course, he wasn't wearing running shorts or shoes."

"I still think it's risky," Eli said. But we could tell he was weakening. "What about Mindy? Think she'll go along with it?"

I nodded. "Yes. She will. We're not saying anything bad about Hoop, or blaming him for anything." I stood up. "I think we should go to the hospital right now and see if they've found out who he is. If they haven't, we have to tell them."

Bay and Eli stood up. "Maybe they already know," Bay said, hope in his voice. "That way, we could just turn around and leave without having to say anything at all."

"That wouldn't work," Nat said. "The minute they know who he is, the police are going to start asking questions around campus. Like who Hoop's closest friends are, for instance. The police will come knocking at our doors to find out where we were tonight. It'll be better for us if we mention the argument right now, *before* we're asked. Make sure that everyone knows we weren't with Hoop."

I looked at Nat with a mixture of admiration and revulsion. How easily and well she adapted to the nasty business of hiding information. Then I almost laughed aloud, at myself. "Hiding information?" Didn't I mean "lying?" Something I had once been very, very good at. I had never realized Nat had a talent for lying, too.

Bay drove us to the Twin Falls Medical Center in town. It seemed as we rode up in the elevator to the Intensive Care Unit that anyone looking at us could tell we were guilty of something, as if we had the letters G U I L T Y splattered in red across our chests. None of us said a word. And we were all walking so carefully, almost tiptoeing.

That wasn't guilt. It was fear. We were all terrified of what we were going to find when we got to the ICU.

What we found was a tall, heavyset nurse with gray hair and glasses who told us briskly, "Oh, that burn patient is still being worked on, and from what I saw of him when they brought him in, he won't be seeing any visitors for a long time."

She peered at us from behind her glasses. "Do you think you might know the victim? He hasn't been identified."

I spoke up first. "We think he might be a friend of ours. He was running in the park when the fire broke out."

The nurse sighed. "Well, you're certainly not going to be able to tell by looking at him. The doctors would never let you see him now, and be grateful for that. You wouldn't want to."

I had to clench my teeth, hard, to keep from shaking.

"Still," she went on, "it's imperative that he be identified. His family has to be notified, and we need to know his medical history. If you could give me a description of your friend — height, weight, hair and eye color, that sort of thing — it might help." She took a piece of paper from a notebook on her desk and, pencil poised in the air, looked at us expectantly.

Bay gave her the information, and Eli added, "He has a large, dark mole over his right eyebrow."

The nurse looked at him. "Not anymore, he doesn't," she said brusquely.

I felt my knees give, and clutched at the desk for support.

She apologized immediately. "I'm sorry. I should have been more tactful. What I meant was, serious burns, such as this victim's, erase any identifying marks such as moles or birthmarks or scars. That's all I meant. I didn't mean to upset you. What is your friend's name?"

"Michael," Nat said. "Michael Sinclair. His parents live in Fairlawn, New Jersey."

The nurse held up the piece of paper. "Let me take this in to the doctors and see if the description seems to match. No one else has come forward asking about the fire victim, so he could be your friend. Wait here." She disappeared through a set of double swinging doors.

We didn't sit on the hard blue plastic chairs while we waited. We paced. Up and down the quiet, white-tiled corridor, our shoes making almost no noise. We paced back and forth silently, waiting for the nurse to return and tell us something we didn't want to hear.

The urge to run was overwhelming. I wanted to turn and dash for the elevator and descend quickly and smoothly to the lobby, where I could run outside and all the way back to the campus. That way, I wouldn't have to hear what she said when she returned.

But I didn't run. Running wasn't going to get me out of this one. I could run all the way back home to Rochester and it would still be with me. We were all in it together, me and Nat and Eli, Bay and Mindy . . . and Hoop. Especially Hoop.

So I stayed where I was. But I continued to pace. My shoulder bag made a soft, whispering sound as it swung, repeatedly brushing against my green suede jacket.

The nurse was gone for days, months, years.

When she finally returned, the expression on her face was grim. She signalled to us to return to the desk, then she sat down and looked up at us. "I'm sorry," she said gently. "We believe it is your friend. And," she glanced at Eli and her voice was kind, "the mole is still there, just as you said. It was the only part of his face that — " she stopped, shook her head, said, "well, never mind that now."

"Can we see him?" I asked when I found my voice.

She shook her head. "No, I'm afraid not. You won't be able to see him for quite some time."

"Is he going to make it?" Nat asked.

"We won't know that for a few days. With burns, the danger is of infection, since the skin, which is our protective coating, has been burned away."

Eli went bone-white.

"You should just go home," the nurse added, shuffling a sheaf of papers. "We appreciate your coming in, but there's nothing more you can do here. We'll notify your friend's parents, and I'm sure they'll be grateful that you told us who he was. You can call here anytime to get an update on his condition. Just ask for me, Nurse Lovett." She lifted her head to give us a half-smile, and then focused her attention on her paperwork.

We'd been dismissed.

And we really hadn't learned anything. We still didn't know how seriously Hoop had been burned, although we knew it was bad. We didn't even know if he was going to live.

But we weren't going to learn anything more now.

We walked around the corner to stand by the elevator. "I have to see him," I said in a low voice. "I can't go home until I've seen Hoop."

Bay nodded. "Me, either."

"Lovett can't sit at that desk every single second," Nat said. "And we know where Hoop is. He's behind those double doors."

"Tory," Eli said to me, "you don't want to barge in on those doctors while they're still working on Hoop. From the way the nurse talked, that's not something you want to see."

"He's already been in there a long time," I argued. "They must be almost done by now. By the time that nurse leaves her desk, Hoop could be sleeping in one of the beds back there. We could just sneak in, take a look to see for ourselves that it's him, and then sneak back out again. It'll only take a second."

Because I wasn't the only one who wanted to see with my own eyes that Hoop was alive, no one disagreed, not even Eli. We decided to wait it out, keep a surreptitious eye on Nurse Lovett, and sneak into ICU at the first opportunity.

Our chance didn't come for over an hour. Nurse Lovett was so involved in her paperwork, I thought she'd never leave. Didn't she drink coffee? Didn't she ever go to the bathroom? Wasn't she thirsty? I was so tired, I felt like I might topple over at any second and end up in a hospital bed myself.

Finally, she sat back in her chair, stretched for several seconds, then she stood up. She walked down the hallway and disappeared into a room at the far end.

"Let's go!" I hissed, and we all crept around the corner and through the swinging double doors.

I don't know what I'd expected. I'd never been in an Intensive Care Unit before. A group of doctors, maybe, busily working on Hoop? Or, if the doctors were finished with him for now, maybe there'd be a row of beds lined up side by side, each with a nurse in white in attendance.

It wasn't like that. We walked through the doors and into a large, softly lit, quiet, white area divided into half a dozen windowed cubicles, each with a bed in them. There was no one at the desk in the center of the room.

"There!" Eli whispered, pointing, "the room right beside the nurses' desk."

When I looked, I didn't see how Eli could tell anything from where we stood. All I could see was someone of Hoop's size and bulk lying in a bed. But since the other cubicles closest to us were empty, we all moved apprehensively toward the one Eli had pointed out.

When we got there, we stood peering in through the glass at the figure in the bed.

It didn't look like Hoop. But then, it didn't look like anyone. Completely swathed in white bandages, hooked up to tubes and wires and machines, it lay in the bed unmoving, like an electronic mummy.

It didn't look like a person. And it didn't look alive.

It certainly didn't look like Hoop.

We stood there, not speaking, just staring.

"It's just a body," Nat whispered finally, her hands pressed against the glass. "That's all it is. Just a body." She turned away from the window. I had never seen such sadness on her face. "They said he was alive, but he's not," she added dully. *"That's* not alive." Then her face crumpled, and she cried softly, "What have we done?"

Her words echoed inside my head, making me dizzy. Although Nat was the only one to say it, I knew we were all thinking the same thing.

What had we done?

Chapter 6

"Look," Bay said when we got outside, "can we end the guilt trip right here, please? It was an accident. It's not like we started that fire on purpose. I'm as sorry about Hoop as anyone, but it was just bad luck, that's all."

Nat made a sound of disgust. "Bad luck? Bad *luck*? You're calling what we just looked at upstairs, that . . . that *thing* . . . bad luck?"

Bay spun on his heel and strode to the car, shaking his head. I ran to catch up with him. We stood beside the Bus. I touched his hand. "Nat's upset. We all are. No one's blaming you, Bay. We were *all* there, at the park."

"Yeah, but I was the one who insisted on the fire."

"We could have stopped you, and we didn't." I reached up and put my arms around his neck, hugged him. "We can't make ourselves crazy over this. What good would it do Hoop?"

Nat and Eli arrived. I waited for Nat to say something to Bay, smooth things over, but she didn't. She just climbed into the backseat and huddled silently in a corner.

"Bay's right about one thing," I said when we were on our way back to campus. It was very late. The fire's distant glow had disappeared from the sky, and the streets of Twin Falls were empty. "We can't walk around campus with our heads down and guilt written all over our faces. We're going to be suspected as it is, just because we're Hoop's best friends and it's likely we would have been with him. It's okay to let people know we're upset, because they'll be expecting that. But if we so much as even hint that we were in the park tonight, we can kiss Salem University and our futures good-bye."

"I'm worried about Mindy," Bay said as we left the heart of Twin Falls and headed for the open highway. "She's going to be really shaky. She's nuts about Hoop, we all know that. You add that to the guilt she's going to feel when she finally does see him, and we've got trouble on our hands. What if she tells?"

"If Mindy feels the need to confess," Nat said

dryly from the backseat, "we can just tell her to give her mother a call. A quick conversation with Mrs. I-Was-Miss-Cotton-Ball will remind Mindy that a beauty queen's crown has never been plunked down upon the head of a convicted felon." Nat laughed without humor. "As far as we *know*, anyway."

"I still think you should talk to Mindy," Bay said to me. "Make her see what's at stake here. And keep her away from Hoop if you can. Seeing what we saw tonight could totally unhinge her. Tell her he's recovering nicely but that he's not allowed visitors, and she'll have to be patient. And in the meantime, we need to follow our regular schedules as much as possible. We can't let this throw us."

I nodded. We were passing an off-campus dorm not far from school, an old, red brick house sitting high on a hill overlooking the highway. Nightingale Hall, an off-campus dorm. The kids at school called it *Nightmare* Hall because, according to the stories, some very weird things had happened there. I believed the stories. Nightmare Hall looked like the kind of place where very weird things might happen, especially this late on a moonless night. Tall, gnarled oak trees stood guard over the house, casting ominous shadows across the rolling lawn, and there were no lights on inside.

Ian Banion, the campus radio announcer who had told us a body had been discovered in the fire, lived there. Maybe that's why he'd been able to deliver that horrible news so matter-of-factly, so professionally. Maybe living at Nightmare Hall had taught him that horrible things do happen.

Had it also taught him, I wondered as the house disappeared from sight, what to *do* when horrible things happened?

"You should talk to Mindy first thing in the morning," Bay urged. "Before she has a chance to go to the hospital."

I agreed.

For the second time that night, none of us said good-bye when we separated at the car. I guess we were too lost in our own private misery. But it bothered me that we were all so anxious now to get away from each other. And I knew why. It's not very comfortable being around people who know your worst secret.

I didn't sleep at all, and I know Nat didn't, either. I heard her tossing and turning all night long.

Saturday morning, I called Mindy first thing.

If she saw with her own eyes that Hoop was now nothing more than a body shrouded in white, she'd freak. And if she freaked, anything could slip out of her mouth.

If that happened, we were doomed.

"No visitors," I told her firmly when she answered the phone. "It's for Hoop's sake, Mindy. He'll get better faster if we let the hospital staff take care of him and don't get in their way."

"But I have to *see* him," she protested.

That's because you don't know what you'd be seeing, I thought. If you did . . . "*We* saw him," I said. "And I can tell you that he's being taken care of." That was true enough. "We'd just get in the way if we hung around the hospital. I think you should just do what you always do on the weekend, as if none of this had ever happened."

"What I usually do on the weekend," Mindy burst out, and I could hear tears in her voice, "is hang out with Hoop!"

I swallowed hard. "Why don't we go to the mall," I suggested.

I didn't have anything to do, and I felt sorry for Mindy. Also, it seemed to me that anything would be better than being on campus. I didn't feel like running into people who'd want to talk about what had happened to Hoop.

"You never go to the mall with me, Tory. You always say I take too long to shop."

This was true. I'm not much of a shopper, and Mindy could take hours selecting a pair of black pumps. "Well, I'll make an exception today. Maybe I can talk Nat into going with us."

From her bed, Nat shook her head vigorously. There were faint purple shadows under her eyes. She looked very tired. But I knew I probably did, too.

"Yes," I said firmly into the telephone, "I will definitely drag Nat along. Meet you outside of your sorority house in thirty minutes. Be ready, Mindy. I don't want to have to wait." Her sorority sisters knew Hoop. They'd be ready with questions for Nat and me, questions about last night that I knew we couldn't answer. The faster we got away from the Omega Phi house, the safer I'd feel.

"I'm not going to the mall with you and Mindy," Nat said stubbornly, lying back down in bed. "I'm not going anywhere. I'm just going to lie here all day and see if I can erase the image of Hoop lying in that bed like some petrified Egyptian mummy." She lifted her head and looked at me with anxious eyes. "You don't really think he's going to make it, do you?"

"I don't know," I said, moving to the closet to grab a pair of jeans and a sweater. "But we *are* going to the mall with Mindy. We have to keep her occupied. I don't think I should have to do that all by myself. In fact, I think Bay and Eli should have to come along, too." I turned away from the closet to face Nat. "We're all in this together, Nat, and that's the one thing we can't afford to forget. So get dressed while I call Bay."

When she didn't move, my voice hardened. "I *mean* it, Nat! Get up!"

She did. She was furious, and gave me a look that could melt nails, but she got up, and she dressed, and she left the room with me to meet Bay and Eli. They hadn't wanted to come, either. Eli said, incredulously, "You want to go to the mall *now*?" But when I pointed out that I alone wasn't Mindy's keeper and that they had as much to lose as I did if she talked, they reluctantly agreed to a mall trip.

It turned out to be not such a lousy idea. Away from campus, away from the medical center, away from any reminders of our friend, Hoop Sinclair, we were able to pretend, for a little while, that we'd forgotten about the fire. We teased Mindy about her tendency to waffle for half an hour between a bright red lipstick and another only half a shade lighter. We played pinball in the arcade, and if Bay was slightly off his game, we pretended that was only because he was hungry. To keep pretending, we actually went to the food court and ordered pizza, which lay on our paper plates uneaten while we talked about absolutely nothing.

I was the one who suggested that we all go into the tanning salon with Mindy, who went every week to "refresh her glow." I made it sound as if it could be fun. Mindy was delighted that we were going to join her, something none of us had ever done before. But the truth was, I was afraid that if we left her alone, she'd start spouting her misery to someone in the salon. Maybe tanning salons were like beauty salons, where customers poured out their life secrets like shampoo from an open bottle.

The minute I was inside, though, I regretted my decision. The tanning machines were lidded capsules, self-contained silver boxes on legs, each in a small cubicle with a long, black curtain as a door for privacy. You had to climb inside and close the lid to get your tan.

The capsules were like coffins.

"I'm not getting inside one of those," Nat declared as Mindy made arrangements for all of us at the desk. "Forget it. I'm claustrophobic. Besides, a tan is nothing more than skin damage. Why would I deliberately damage my own skin?"

Eli shuddered, clearly thinking of Hoop's skin under those white bandages. But he said, "We won't be in them that long. Ten minutes, tops. Just keeping Mindy company. How much damage can you get in ten minutes, doctor?"

But Nat was adamant. "Too much. I'll just sit out there in the lobby and read outdated fashion magazines. Don't complain to me if you overdo and end up looking like lobsters. You'll get no sympathy from me." She turned and retreated to the lobby.

The attendant explained to the rest of us the safety features of the tanning machines, how this latch worked and that little gizmo flipped sideways, and then she showed us how the controls worked. When she thought we had it all down pat, she gave us clean, white wraparound towels to wear, and left us, each with our own separate cubicle and silver-lidded box.

"Watch the timers," Mindy warned us before getting into her own tanning machine. "Especially you, Tory. You're so fair-skinned. Don't fall asleep or anything, or you'll be sorry."

I had no intention of falling asleep inside the

silver coffin, even though a nap would have felt good. I was very, very tired.

I drew the curtain on my booth, undressed, and, wrapped in my towel, climbed into my capsule. I set the timer carefully for only ten minutes, just long enough to take away my guilty pallor. Then I closed the lid and my eyes, and warned myself not to doze off. Even if I did, the timer would buzz when the ten minutes were up, waking me.

There was a dim, rosy glow inside the box, and I found it soothing. The surface I was lying on was firm, but not uncomfortable, and I felt my skin warming gently under the lights. A tan in March might be nice, after all, I decided. I'd look good with a nice, healthy glow. Maybe the fatigued, guilty look would go away and I'd look vibrant and very much alive. And innocent.

But I must have dozed off, after all, because I never did hear the timer go off. I just all of a sudden became conscious that the sound of that timer steadily ticking away the minutes had ended.

I opened my eyes.

The tanning lights were still on.

But the timer was at zero. Ten minutes, at least, had passed. I wasn't wearing a watch and couldn't be sure just how much time had passed, but my skin was beginning to feel hot and dry.

I couldn't sit up because of the closed lid. But the attendant had carefully explained to us how to turn the lid lever sideways to push it open.

I was getting very warm. Beads of sweat dampened my bangs.

I reached up, turned the lever, pushed on the lid to open it.

Nothing happened.

The lid didn't open.

I pushed again, harder this time. Sweat beaded my upper lip.

The lid remained in place.

I used both hands, pushing with all of my strength. I put my back muscles to work, my shoulders, pushing, pushing, grunting with the effort, pushing, pushing . . .

The lid refused to open.

Now, I could feel my skin burning. Remembering Mindy's warning, I knew how important it was that I get free of the tanning capsule.

But I couldn't.

I was trapped.

Chapter 7

While I continued pushing with all my might, I tried to control my panic enough to remember what the attendant had told us about the failsafe controls located inside the capsule. A button, she'd said. There was supposed to be a small, red button I could push to set off an alarm if something went wrong. Something had definitely gone wrong. Where *was* that button?

There! There it was sitting right in the middle of the lid.

I stabbed it.

And waited.

Nothing happened. No one yanked the lid open and set me free.

My skin felt as if I were being roasted over a campfire, like the hot dogs from the night before.

I jabbed the button again, and at the same

time, I yelled. At the top of my lungs. And once I started yelling, I couldn't stop. I screamed for Mindy, for Bay, for Eli, for Nat. I even yelled Hoop's name, forgetting.

My screams bounced around uselessly inside the capsule, and no one came.

The tanning lights were supposed to go off when the timer did. That's what the attendant had told us would happen. Then she had said that if they didn't, an alarm would go off and she would hear it, and if *that* didn't happen, we could push the red button ourselves to summon help.

Not only had my alarm not gone off, neither had my tanning "rays." I couldn't tell what color my skin was under their pinkish glow, but I had a sinking feeling from the way my face and arms felt, that I was already lobster-red, just as Nat had predicted. My skin felt potato-chip crisp, as if every last bit of moisture had been sucked from it. And my face was beginning to hurt.

Breathing hard, I gave up on the lid and lay back down in the capsule. My head ached, and my skin felt as if it were too small for my body, as if it might split at any second and I'd explode like the hot dog Nat had left on her stick too long last night.

Eventually, I knew, my friends, free of their own capsules, would realize that I wasn't with them. They would come, then, to set me free.

But what would my skin look like by then? I'd been told the same horror stories about sun damage that the rest of my generation had. I'd stopped lying out in the backyard during the summer three years earlier. I didn't want to look ninety years old when I was only sixty, and I didn't want skin cancer, and I especially didn't want ugly, oozing blisters, which was what a friend of mine in high school had had when she'd fallen asleep at the beach. What a disgusting mess she'd been for weeks afterward.

I did *not* want that.

Spurred on by the image of my friend's blistered, oozing back and shoulders, I lifted my legs and flung them at the lid, kicking with as much force as I could muster. The skin on my thighs felt so dry and stiff, I half-expected to hear ripping sounds as I kicked out.

The lid didn't fly open, as I'd hoped. And I heard nothing from outside. Nothing.

So I kicked again, harder this time. The capsule shook with the force of the blow. But what good did that do me? Even if my silver prison had shaken so visibly on its metal legs, no one would have seen it. Each capsule was hidden behind a black velvet curtain.

I realized then that the ventilation system wasn't working any better than the lid latch or the red button. Because the tanning salon wasn't out to suffocate anyone, there was air in the capsules. At least, there was supposed to be. But my chest hurt and my head ached. Breathing was becoming very difficult.

This whole capsule had malfunctioned and if I didn't do something, I was going to be seriously malfunctioning, too.

I didn't have a whole lot of choices. Yelling hadn't worked, kicking at the lid had done no good at all, and it wasn't as if I could pick up a telephone and call for help.

I began doing the only thing I could think of . . . throwing myself against the side of the capsule in an effort to tip it over. Maybe if the capsule crashed to the ground, the impact would force the lid open, like a car door flying open when hit by another car.

And even if that didn't happen, if I was successful and the capsule tipped over onto the floor, someone would hear the noise, wouldn't they?

I was using every ounce of concentration I had to keep from screaming. Now, I switched that concentration and energy into throwing myself with all my might repeatedly against the side of the capsule.

I only weigh a hundred and ten pounds. But I was angry and frantic for air, and desperate. After three or four hefty tries, I felt the capsule shaking vigorously. After two more slams against the wall, it tipped slightly. Two more, which hurt my burning skin, and it teetered precariously. I was afraid of what would happen to me in the impact when the capsule hit the ground, but I was a lot more terrified of either suffocating or burning to a crisp. So I kept slamming my body sideways.

I became completely caught up in my frantic ritual and wasn't really thinking anymore. Just rolling to one side and then heaving myself back in the other direction to slam against the wall, then repeating the motion over and over again.

When the capsule finally went over, I wasn't prepared.

When it toppled over slowly and heavily and slammed on its side onto the tiled floor, the blow dazed my overheated brain and it took me a few seconds to understand that I had succeeded. Another few to notice that the lid had indeed snapped open and that I was staring straight into the back wall of my cubicle.

Gasping for breath and shaking my head to clear it, I crawled slowly, painfully, out of the tanning capsule.

And saw someone's leg darting through the black curtain.

Aside from the fact that no one else should have been in my cubicle — because if they had been, why hadn't they helped me — there was something else about the leg that stunned me. It wasn't wearing jeans or shorts or a skirt and it wasn't bare, as if the person it belonged to had been tanning. Instead, it was wrapped, from the bottom of the foot to the top of the knee, which was all I caught a glimpse of, in thick white bandages.

Like a mummy.

Those tanning rays must have done something to my brain.

A minute later, the curtain was pulled aside and Bay stood there, looking down at me in disbelief. His face, I noticed, was nicely bronzed. But then, he'd probably been able to leave his capsule at exactly the right moment. Unlike me.

"What are you doing on the floor?" he asked. "What happened to your capsule?" Then, "Hey, Tory, you're red as a beet! What's going on?"

Good question.

I wasn't crying or sobbing or hysterical when he helped me out of the booth. I cried out once when he touched my beet-red shoulder, but that was all. If I'd been thinking about what had almost happened to me, I probably would have been screaming.

But it wouldn't be until much, much later that I would start shaking as the impact of what had happened sank in.

For now, the question still was, Why had I been inside that capsule for so long? What had gone wrong?

We mulled that over on the way back to campus. The attendant had insisted repeatedly, in a slightly snide tone of voice, that there was no way the alarm wouldn't have gone off had I actually been locked inside the capsule. She seemed to be saying that I'd only pretended to be locked in.

As if anyone would do something so stupid.

To get attention, she hinted.

Oh, yeah, sure. Wouldn't we all risk serious burns and horrible pain just to get attention? I may not be the most noticeable person in the world, but I'd have to be seriously insane to choose second-degree burns all over my body as a way of standing out in a crowd.

"You could have ended up in the hospital!" the attendant said, her upper lip curling slightly as she frantically checked and double-checked all the wiring, the levers, the buttons, on my capsule. "Don't you realize how danger-ous overdoing it can be? If you've broken this capsule, you'll have to pay for it."

She could find nothing wrong with the cap-sule. She also found no sign of malfunction.

Worse than anything was that I wasn't even sure my friends believed me.

"I couldn't get out," I repeated when we were in the car. "I tried. I pushed and kicked and shoved, but that lid was not about to move. Something was wrong with it."

"You look like a lobster," Nat said from the backseat. "I *told* you you would. Why didn't you listen to me?"

Exactly what I was asking myself. "I also pushed the alarm button," I insisted. "Nothing happened."

"The attendant checked it," Bay said. "Couldn't find anything wrong with it. You sure you're okay?"

No, I was definitely not okay. I'd been re-moved from the hot coals a few minutes too late. My entire body was on fire, and inside, I was shaking. I wondered if I was going to blister.

And then I thought of Hoop.

What I was feeling now, he had to be feeling ten thousand times worse.

"I want to go to the hospital," I said suddenly.

"You feel that bad?" Eli asked, alarm in his voice. He'd changed his mind and left his capsule after two minutes, and like Nat, had no tan, although his cheekbones had a nice glow to them. Mindy didn't have any color, either. She admitted that once inside the booth she'd changed her mind, and just lay there, thinking about Hoop.

"No, I don't feel that bad," I answered Eli. "But I want to see Hoop."

"We can't," he reminded me. "They won't let us."

"We're his best friends, Eli," I said through stiff, stinging lips. I turned to Bay. "Please. Just for a few minutes. Maybe he's much better."

"Tory, I want to see Hoop, too," Mindy said, leaning over the front seat. "But you really should go to the infirmary and get something for your sunburn."

I'd forgotten that Mindy was with us. There went my visit to Hoop. We could not take Mindy to the hospital. The minute she saw that her handsome, athletic boyfriend had become a mummy, she'd freak. She'd probably start shrieking wildly that it was our fault, all our fault.

We couldn't risk that.

"Okay, Mindy's right," I said hastily before Bay could turn the car toward the Medical Center. "We wouldn't be allowed to see Hoop, anyway. Take me to the infirmary instead, please, Bay."

I'd go back to see Hoop later, by myself.

"What *do* you think happened back there at the salon?" Eli asked me quietly. "I mean, any ideas about why you couldn't get out of that capsule?"

"The lid was probably just stuck," Bay interjected. "The attendant said that happens sometimes. That's why they have the alarm buttons inside the lid."

"It wasn't stuck," I disagreed. "I'm not as puny as I look. If it was just stuck, I could have kicked it open. And even if it was stuck, that doesn't explain why the alarm button didn't work. Did you see that wire leading from the top of the lid to the button? It looked like it would have been really easy to disconnect it. The ventilation system stopped working, too. I could have suffocated."

"Tory!" Nat's voice. "What are you saying?"

"I'm saying," I said firmly, "that I don't think I was accidentally trapped inside that capsule. If the attendant wants to believe it was my own fault because she's terrified of a lawsuit, let her. But I'm telling you, someone, somehow, trapped me in that thing and disconnected the alarm button on purpose."

Once I'd said the words aloud, I realized that I'd believed it from that first, scary moment when the lid wouldn't open.

They all fell silent, thinking about what I'd just said.

I knew how bizarre it sounded. But there were so many switches, so many gizmos, so many levers on that capsule, any one of them could have been tampered with.

Then I remembered that I'd seen someone darting out of my cubicle.

"Did any of you guys see someone with a bandaged leg walk by while you were waiting in the lobby?" I asked.

"A bandaged leg?" Nat thought for a second. "No. Tory, why would someone with a bandaged leg be getting a tan? Wouldn't they look a little silly when the bandages came off and one leg was tan and one wasn't? What a question."

I'd been upset, almost hysterical when I crawled out of that capsule. How could I be sure of what I'd seen? If anyone had been in that cubicle, bandaged or not, they would have seen that I was in trouble, and let me out.

So, when Nat said after a minute or two, "Tory? You really think someone locked you in that capsule on purpose?" I did a complete about-face.

"No, no, of course not," I said hastily. "That's a really crazy idea. I guess those tanning rays must have melted my brain. I'm sure the attendant was right. I must have pushed the wrong button, turned the wrong lever, whatever. Forget it. Maybe the doctor at the infirmary can give me something for my brain meltdown, too."

Relief filled the car. They'd been as repelled as I was by the idea of someone deliberately locking me in that capsule. Didn't we already have enough to worry about?

"Mindy," I said, changing the subject, "we need to fill you in on the story we're going to tell everyone about last night." I told her what we'd made up, about Hoop running off in a flash of anger.

At first, she balked. "That's like blaming Hoop!" she cried. "It's like saying it was his temper that put him in the hospital. That's not true, and it's not fair."

"May I remind you," I said icily, "that it was your idea not to go back and look for him? That you were the one who insisted that Hoop would be just fine on his own in that fire?"

Mindy let out a dismayed gasp. So did Nat, and I could feel Eli's questioning eyes on my face.

I hated myself.

But it was true, wasn't it? Mindy knew Hoop better than any of us, and she had insisted he'd be okay. Well, she'd been wrong, hadn't she?

If it crossed my mind that she was probably being tortured by the same exact thought, I ignored it. It was more important now that Mindy go along with the story we'd made up than to worry about her feelings. We couldn't let her ruin everything.

"Look, everyone knows that Hoop has a temper," I said patiently, even though what I really felt like doing was screaming. My skin burned fiercely, I was still upset about having been locked in that capsule, and I wanted all of this horror over Hoop to disappear. I didn't feel like dealing with Mindy. But if she caved in and told anyone the truth, we were all dead. "No one will question our story, Mindy. People have seen him lose his temper too many times."

I'll never know whether or not my comments changed Mindy's mind, or if what happened next changed it for her. Because when we arrived back on campus, the place was crawling with cops. There were black-and-whites lined up outside the administration building, Butler Hall, and a couple of official-looking cars with the state logo on the doors, plus two brown and cream state police cars. Everywhere we looked, there seemed to be people in uniform, on the walkways, on the Commons, going in and out of the dorms.

Bay drove slowly, as we all stared in apprehension.

"I thought Twin Falls had a tiny police force," Nat murmured.

"They're not all Twin Falls," Eli said. "Some are state police, some are campus security, and I think the guys in white shirts and navy blue pants might be arson investigators. It's a state park, remember? The fire isn't just a local matter."

Mindy groaned, and leaning over the front seat again, said quickly, "Okay, okay, I'll go with that story."

My stiff, aching body went weak with relief.

The doctor at the infirmary said I wouldn't blister. She shook her head in disapproval at what she called "youthful vanity," and warned me away from the tanning salon. As if that was necessary.

She told me I was "a very lucky young woman," gave me a tube of salve to apply to the most painful spots, and dismissed me.

It was Saturday. I hadn't spent a Saturday night alone since I'd met Eli, and then Bay and the others. But when we separated at Devereaux, no one said a word about doing anything that night, not even Bay. I could have leaned in through the open car window after I got out and said, "See you tonight?" but something wouldn't let me. The fire had damaged more than the park and Hoop. It had done something to our little group, too. Our easy, trusting attitude toward each other was gone.

Maybe we were all just too shell-shocked to think about going out and having fun. Whatever the reason, Nat and I got out of the car without saying good-bye. All I said as I left was, "Remember, Mindy, don't screw this up, okay?"

She nodded, but she looked hurt.

"That was kind of mean," Nat commented as we went inside. "She already promised that she'd go along with the story."

"I know. It *was* mean. But the police are going to be coming around and she's our weakest link. She can't stand the thought of lying about Hoop. I don't like it, either, so if you have any better suggestions that will get us out of this mess, I'd be happy to hear them."

We rode upstairs in the elevator in silence.

To find two uniformed Twin Falls officers and one state police officer waiting for us in the hall outside our room.

Chapter 8

The first question was directed at me. "What happened to your face?" the younger of the two Twin Falls officers asked as we ushered them all into our room. "Looks like you burned it some. How?"

I explained. I didn't want to. It sounded hopelessly stupid even to me, and I'd *been* there. But I was afraid that if I didn't explain, they'd assume my face had been seared by the forest fire, proof that I'd been with Hoop. So I had to tell them. I didn't even hint that I was suspicious about how it had happened, though — that would have kept them there longer, and I just wanted them to go away.

I found myself wishing our room were neater, as if that would convince the officers that we were fine, upstanding citizens. Then again, a perfectly neat dorm room would probably have made them even more suspicious.

"I imagine your friend, the basketball player who was injured in the park fire, hurts a lot worse than you do," the older officer said sternly, moving forward, small notebook in hand. "Could we ask you about that, please?"

That's when I realized that we'd made one big mistake when we decided on the "story" we'd be telling. We had decided that we would say Hoop had lost his temper and run off in the direction of the state park.

But what we *hadn't* discussed was what *we* were supposed to have been doing when the fire started, and where, exactly, we were doing it. How could we have neglected to come up with those very important details?

Those were the first questions we were asked.

Nat and I looked at each other as if someone had just asked us to describe the Pythagorean theory.

I began stammering an answer before she did. "Well, uh, we were . . . we were *here* when Hoop took off. Right . . . right here, in this room."

"And after that?" the officer asked, his eyes never leaving my face for a second. "Where were you the rest of the night?"

I couldn't think. With him looking at me like that, my brain balked. Count me out of this one, it said, and promptly ceased to function. Suddenly brainless, all I could manage was, "Here. We . . . we stayed here."

His eyebrows rose sharply. "You stayed here in the dorm room on a night when everyone else was out celebrating Salem's win in the semifinals?"

"Well, we didn't stay here the *whole* night," Nat said, coming to my rescue. "We thought you meant where were we when the fire started. We were here," she lied easily. "But then we went out."

"To?" His eyebrows were still arched, fat, furry caterpillars inching toward his hairline.

Instantly, I felt Nat's dilemma. If she said we'd gone to Vinnie's or Johnny's, or any one of a dozen other hangouts, the police would make the rounds, asking if we'd been there.

"Down by the river," she said. "We took some sandwiches and went down and sat on the riverbank." She'd thought fast enough to substitute sandwiches for our hot dogs. Hot dogs required a fire. It was absolutely essential that we not be associated with fire in any way.

"Anyone see you there?" the state police officer asked. He was big and burly, could have used a uniform one size larger than the one he was poured into, and his tie was crooked. But his voice was gentle as he asked the question.

"Gee, I don't think so," Nat said, pretending to think about it for a minute. "We didn't see anyone, did we, Tory?"

"No. Not a soul." I looked directly into the eyes of the policeman who had asked me the first question. "We wanted to have our own private celebration. That's what we argued with Hoop about," I added, improvising as I talked. "He wanted to go where the crowd was, and we didn't."

Mistake. I thought I was being so clever, volunteering information that would fortify our story. But I was underestimating the intelligence of our questioners.

"He wanted to be where there was a crowd, so he opted for running alone in the state park?" the state police officer said skeptically. "Seems to me he'd have gone on into town to find his crowd."

"Not without Mindy, he wouldn't have," Nat said hastily. "That's his girlfriend, Mindy Loomis. And she was here, with us."

My elbow made its way into Nat's ribs. She shouldn't have mentioned Mindy. Mindy was so shaky. Liable to say almost anything.

"So what you're saying," the younger officer said, pencil poised on his notepad, "is that you weren't anywhere near the park last night?"

Oh, damn. There it was. Talking about lying to the authorities is one thing. Now that I actually had to *do* it, I couldn't. I'd done it before, in high school. It had never worked. I wasn't very good at it and something always tripped me up.

"Well, like we said," Nat said, saving me again, "we were on the riverbank. I guess you could say that's near the park, right?" Her eyes had never looked more innocent. "We wouldn't want to mislead you, officers."

What could they say? I wasn't sure they believed us, but they couldn't prove that we were lying, so they left, telling us they might be back and to "be available."

"That means," I said as I closed the door after them, "don't leave town. Funny, since we're only lying so that we can *stay*. If we wanted to leave town, all we'd have to do is spill our guts and the administration and the townspeople and the police would be only too happy to escort us out of town. We should write a book: *How to Go from College to Prison in One Easy Move*."

Nat was shaking. "You shouldn't have said

we were here last night," she accused. "What a dumb thing to say! Like we'd be sitting around the room while everyone else was out celebrating. Who'd believe that?"

"Well, you shouldn't have mentioned Mindy, either," I snapped. "They're probably heading for her room right this minute. What if she folds?"

"Oh, you sound like someone in a bad movie." Nat flopped down on her bed and buried her face in her pillow. "She's not going to 'fold.' She's not giving up everything now. She's as determined as any of the rest of us."

I hoped Nat was right.

I had just slathered a greasy coating of salve onto my stiff, aching, skin when Bay called.

"A lot of people are really ticked about the fire," he informed me, speaking in a low voice. There must have been someone else in his room at the Quad. "They've closed the whole park, even the sections that didn't burn. There was supposed to be a ten-K run through there tomorrow. Had to be cancelled. And a bunch of people had planned a midnight picnic there tonight. That's cancelled, too. No fishing allowed off the riverbank, either, until the arson investigators come up with some answers."

I groaned silently. We really had screwed

up. For just a second there, I hated Bay with a fierce passion. He was the one who had insisted that we make a campfire. If he hadn't been so stubborn, so insistent, none of this would have happened.

But we could have voted Bay down, and we hadn't.

"Then there's Hoop," Bay continued into my silence. "Everyone's really bummed about Hoop. We had a good chance at taking the finals. But without him, we're lost."

Of course there would be no way Hoop could play. The game was Tuesday night. We didn't even know if he would live until Tuesday night. And no one had to tell us that if he had a future at all, it wouldn't be in sports. He'd be lucky if he ever walked again, never mind running up and down a basketball court.

"So everyone's mad about that, too, although they don't come right out and say so. They know that thinking about a trophy sounds pretty shallow when they should be thinking about Hoop. But you can see it in their eyes: kiss the championship good-bye."

Everyone hated us. Only they didn't *know* it was *us* they hated. They just hated whoever had been stupid and careless enough to start that fire.

I did, too.

Bay wanted me to meet him, just to talk for a little while.

I said no. I knew he wanted me to make him feel better. We'd sit on the Commons somewhere and tell each other that we hadn't meant it, we'd blame the high wind and the dry winter, we'd say that it could have happened to anyone. And then maybe we'd hold each other and kiss and try to make it all disappear.

But it wouldn't disappear.

Besides, I had something else I wanted to do, and I didn't want Bay to know. He'd disapprove, and try to talk me out of it.

So I told him my burned skin hurt too much and I was going to go to bed.

And I did. Nat and I both did.

I waited for her to fall asleep. It took forever, and I almost dozed off myself.

As soon as I was positive that she was really out, I got up quietly, threw on a pair of jeans, sweater, sneakers and jacket, and left the room.

Chapter 9

I drove myself to the hospital. The secondhand maroon Escort that my parents had given me as a reward for being accepted at Salem wasn't as flashy or as new as Hoop's Miata or as useful as Bay's car, but I liked it. It got me where I wanted to go, although most of the time I took the shuttle because it was free.

But there would be people on the shuttle. They'd want to know why my face looked like someone had taken a torch to it, and they'd ask all kinds of questions about Hoop.

Who needed that?

Almost from the moment I slid behind the wheel, I had this weird, creepy sensation along the back of my neck. I had checked the backseat before I got in, as I always did, and there hadn't been any maniacs in ski masks lying there, hiding under a blanket. So why the feeling, as I drove off campus, that someone's eyes were boring a hole through the back of my head?

There *were* cars behind me as I pulled out onto the highway, but that didn't mean someone was following me. It was Saturday evening. Everyone was going out. If it hadn't been for last night, I'd be with them: Mindy and Hoop, Eli and Nat, Bay and I, would be headed downtown to Johnny's or to a movie at the mall, or maybe to a party at Nightmare Hall. The place was creepy, but they threw great parties there.

Even on the open highway, the feeling of being watched didn't fade. I kept glancing into my rearview mirror, but all I could see were headlights.

Quit being paranoid, I told myself, and concentrated on driving. In spite of the salve, my burned skin still felt parchment-dry, and I ached every time I turned the wheel.

When I reached the Medical Center, I went directly to ICU. Stepping out of the elevator, I found two people sitting in the tiny waiting area. A large, balding man was asleep in a chair, an open magazine in his lap. A small, gray-haired woman sipping coffee sat opposite him, her eyes staring at the white tiled floor. She'd been crying.

I knew who they were from Parents' Day. Hoop's folks. I clenched my teeth. I did *not* want to talk to them. Was I going to be able to slip by unseen? Mr. Sinclair was no problem, sitting there with his eyes closed, but what if Hoop's mother looked up? She might remember me, and want to talk. I knew I wasn't up to that.

I stepped back into the elevator, returned to the lobby, and took the fire stairs back up to ICU.

Halfway there, I thought I heard footsteps below me, but decided it was my imagination. And even if it wasn't, why shouldn't other people be using the stairs? I kept going.

I came out of the stairs at a safe distance from the waiting area and waited behind a tall, potted plant until Nurse Lovett left her post. Then I scurried into the ICU unit and went straight to Hoop's window.

He wasn't there.

The bed was empty.

They had said he might not make it through the first seventy-two hours. And his mother had been crying . . .

I almost lost it right then and there; until my brain said, Get a grip, Tory. Would Hoop's father be taking a nice, restful snooze if his son had just died?

Of course not. What was wrong with me?

I went back out to the desk and waited for Nurse Lovett.

"You're not supposed to be here," she said sharply when she returned and saw me standing there. "Only immediate family. What happened to your face?"

"Where's Hoop?" I demanded, ignoring her question about my face. None of her business. And I made no apology for the fact that I wasn't related to Hoop. I still had a right to be there, whether she thought so or not.

She must have remembered me from the night before because she didn't say, "Who? Oh, you mean the Sinclair boy, Michael." Sitting down at her desk, she said instead, "He's back now. He was down on the second floor. Consultation about his course of treatment." She looked up at me. "It's going to be very rough, you know. If he makes it at all, there will be times during his recovery when he'll wish he hadn't. Treatment for burns as serious as his is horribly painful. He's going to need a lot of support. I hope you'll continue to come and see him through the long haul. Most people can't take it and give up after a while."

Well, I thought but didn't say, I'd like to be here for Hoop, but *he* may have something to say about that. Because when he is alert and recovering, he's going to remember exactly what happened. And maybe he'll hate the five people who were once his very best friends, because they didn't come back and save him from that fire. So he probably won't want to see our faces.

"Has he said anything yet?" I asked.

Nurse Lovett shook her head. "Oh, heavens no. He couldn't possibly talk. His face . . . well, he hasn't even been conscious yet. Be grateful for small favors. In fact, it's really senseless for you to keep making these trips down here. It's going to be a while before he's physically able to talk, and even longer before he'll feel like making the attempt. Just call. We'll keep you updated on his condition."

I knew she was right. It really *didn't* make much sense to keep going to the medical center when Hoop was still in such bad shape.

But I wanted, *needed*, to see him one more time before I left. I waited until Nurse Lovett's back was turned, and then did an end run around her. In the ICU unit, I went to Hoop's window and stood looking in at him.

I don't know what I'd been hoping for. A miracle, maybe. To see Hoop, unbandaged, sitting up in bed, watching a basketball game on television and scarfing down hospital food.

No such luck. There was no sign of life at all in the white-wrapped figure lying motionless in the white hospital bed with tubes running in and out of his body. That's all it seemed to be from where I stood, a body. It could as easily have been a mannequin from one of the department stores in Twin Falls.

The sight sickened me. The Hoop I'd known and liked, even loved as a friend, had been replaced by this mannequinlike, lifeless figure.

At least, I tried to tell myself, he wasn't screaming in agony.

"Excuse me," a soft voice said from behind me, "but aren't you Tory Alexander? One of Michael's friends?"

I groaned silently. Hoop's mother. I should have beat it out of there the minute I'd seen the empty bed.

I turned around. What else could I do?

"Hi, Mrs. Sinclair." She looked terrible. Her blouse and skirt were wrinkled, there was a small coffee stain on one blouse pocket, and her gray hair needed combing. And I had never seen such sad eyes. "You really should be sleeping, like your husband."

"Oh, I can't sleep," she said, taking my hand to lead me into the waiting room. The lights were brighter in there and when she turned to look at me, she looked confused. "Tory? Were you . . . you weren't with Michael in that terrible fire, were you? I thought the rangers told us he was alone in the park. But your face . . ."

"Oh, this," I said, waving a hand. "No, I screwed up at the tanning salon today."

She looked even more confused. I knew what she was thinking. She was thinking, My Michael is lying in a hospital bed in agony, teetering on the edge of death, and one of his best friends went to a tanning salon? I will never understand young people if I live to be a thousand.

I didn't like what she was thinking, but it would have taken too long to explain. "I'm sorry about Hoop, Mrs. Sinclair. I know how worried you must be. But he'll be fine," I added lamely.

Her faded blue eyes clouded. "I keep thinking that any minute now, they'll come out and tell us that it isn't really Michael in there, that they're terribly sorry, but they made a mistake. It's some other unfortunate person lying in that bed all wrapped in bandages and hooked up to machines, and Michael is right this moment eating dinner at that lovely Chinese restaurant in town."

"Hunan Manor," I murmured absentmindedly. She wasn't letting go of my hand.

"Yes, that's the one. You know, it really doesn't *look* like Michael in that bed, don't you agree, Tory?"

I wasn't cruel enough to say that it didn't look like *anyone*. "I'm sure he's going to be okay," I mumbled again.

But we both knew he wasn't. Not "okay" as in he'd be racing up and down a basketball court any day now, and not "okay" as in, he'd be dancing up a storm at Johnny's by next Saturday night, and not "okay" as in, he would eventually be as handsome and unblemished as he once was. Michael "Hoop" Sinclair wasn't ever going to be that kind of okay again, and his mother and I knew it.

Before she could ask the question I'd been dreading — "How did this happen to my son, Tory?" — I said for a third time that I was sure he'd be okay, muttered something about having to study for a test (on Saturday night?

Mrs. Sinclair must have been thinking), and ran for the elevator.

And even though she was no longer looking at me when the doors closed, even though she'd returned to her husband's side and was instead looking down at him as if she wished desperately that he'd wake up so she wouldn't be alone, I could still feel the incredible sadness in her eyes, and knew that I would for a very long time.

But it wasn't *her* eyes that troubled me as I hurried the two blocks to my car. Her eyes were sad and bleak and lonely. I still felt eyes on my back, and they felt . . . *angry*. An angry stare burned into the back of my neck. I knew I was being ridiculous . . . there was no one around. No sound of footsteps, either. But I could *feel* those eyes on me . . .

I tried to shake the feeling. At least half a dozen times on my way to the car I stopped, my heart woodpeckering away in my chest, and turned to peer into the darkness. And saw . . . nothing. Absolutely nothing but the brightly lit medical center, the trees and bushes surrounding it. No one was following me.

Still, I had never been so glad to unlock the door of the Escort and slip inside, quickly relocking the door. I didn't even take the time to check the backseat. But, remembering my mother's repeated warnings, I did check before I left the parking lot. Nothing there but a pile of books and an old sweater that I'd always hated.

Wherever the watching "eyes" were coming from, it wasn't the backseat of my car.

Still glancing repeatedly into my rearview mirror, I had just left the business district of Twin Falls, when a tiny red light suddenly began blinking at me from the dashboard.

I had no idea what it meant, but it had never been on before and I knew it wasn't supposed to be on now.

All I wanted to do was get safely back to campus and run to my room. I kept going, hoping that the little red light didn't mean anything important and thinking that even if it did, sheer force of will might keep the car going long enough to get me back to campus.

I was wrong, on both counts.

The light stopped blinking after a few minutes and became instead a steady, burning red glow, staring at me accusingly.

I kept going.

And then the car began chugging, something it had never done before.

A minute or two later, just as I was approaching gloomy old Nightmare Hall on my right, a terrifying sight met my eyes. There was a thin stream of smoke trailing out from under the hood of my car.

Then, just as quickly, it wasn't a thin stream, but a wide plume, which in seconds became a thick, gray cloud pouring out into the dark night air.

I stared at it, transfixed.

My car was on fire.

Chapter 10

If I hadn't panicked, I would never have been stupid enough to open the hood. But the highway was deserted, there was no one I could flag down to tell me what to do, that creepy old house on the hill was staring down at me, and I guess I went a little crazy with fear.

I turned off the ignition, jumped from the car and ran around to the front to yank the hood open. I don't know what I was thinking. Maybe in my terror and temporary madness I thought opening the hood would keep the car from exploding into a huge ball of flame and smoke.

Or maybe I wasn't thinking at all.

One second later, the air was filled with screams of agony. They were *my* screams, as hot steam scalded my already-seared face. Too late, my hands flew to cover my face and, screaming, I staggered backward to escape the heat.

The pain was excruciating. I couldn't stop screaming, couldn't stand in one place, kept running back and forth, back and forth, my hands over my face, my mouth letting go of one piercing scream after another.

No one in the house on the hill above me heard my screams. The door didn't open, no one rushed down the gravel driveway to help me.

But there *was* help up there. There had to be. Someone had to be home, someone to make this terrible pain go away, someone to take me back to the safety of my room on campus.

Because I still felt someone was after me. And I felt so vulnerable standing there alone on the side of the road.

When the excruciating pain eased a little, I let my hands drop from my face and looked up at the house. There seemed to be only a few lights on inside the house. The branches of the huge old oak trees were still bare, their branches pointing like wizened fingers toward the moonless sky. I heard no music coming from the house, no voices or laughter. But someone *had* to be inside, I told myself.

I did *not* want to go up to that house. I'd

been in it once or twice, at parties, and I'd had a good time. But I could remember thinking then that being inside Nightmare Hall while a party was going on, while there were people and music and laughter and talk and dancing, had to be very different from being there late at night when the lights were off and all was quiet. Nothing to distract you then from hearing the eerie sounds the huge, drafty old house must make or from seeing things in the shadows that you didn't want to see.

If I hadn't been in so much trouble, I would never have trudged up that curving gravel driveway. But I had no choice. My footsteps as I reluctantly climbed the hill crunched softly. The only other sound was my pained breathing.

The porch light wasn't on, and I had only the faint light from several windows to guide my way. But even in that dim glow, I could see that the porch tilted slightly, as if the posts holding it up were different lengths, and the tired black shutters could have used a coat of paint. An old wooden swing moved slightly as the oak tree branches overhead tossed a brisk breeze toward the house.

The breeze moved the swing gently backward, toward the white railing, and then forward again before allowing it to settle into place.

That was when I noticed that it wasn't empty.

My knees went weak with relief. Someone *was* home, after all. I wouldn't even have to go inside Nightmare Hall to get help because here they were, sitting outside, almost as if they'd been waiting for me.

Waiting for me?

If they'd been sitting on that swing for more than a few minutes, they had to have heard my screams. I was surprised that the people *inside* the house, if there were any, hadn't come rushing out, my screaming had seemed so shrill and loud. It would have been impossible for anyone sitting outside on that swing not to have heard me.

Then why hadn't they rushed down the hill to help?

There was something else odd about the figure sitting on the swing.

It was dressed all in white.

I moved closer but slowly, cautiously, still wondering why whoever this was hadn't come to help me.

Suddenly I had that feeling again, the feeling of eyes on me, watching me, angry and filled with hate. It hit me like a hammer to my chest, so strong, so powerful that it took my breath away.

I stopped walking, I stopped breathing, I stopped wondering, but my eyes remained fixated on the figure in the swing.

And then I realized why he or she appeared to be dressed all in white. Because of the bandages.

The figure on the swing was completely swathed in bandages, from the top of its head, around its head and face, down its neck and shoulders, arms, chest, legs, and feet. The only visible parts of its body were its eyes, staring out from between the wide, white strips of gauze.

My mouth fell open, and my breath caught in my throat. Hoop. It looked exactly like Hoop sitting there.

It couldn't. This . . . thing . . . wasn't Hoop. It was something else. Had to be. But . . . *what*?

I couldn't see the expression in its eyes, but I could *feel* it. Hatred . . . undiluted, raw hatred. I felt it as surely and as strongly as if we were only inches apart and I was staring directly into its face.

It stood up, stiffly, like an automaton, and,

arms swinging at its sides, began moving away from the swing. Toward *me*. I heard a hoarse, whispery voice utter one word. "Tory," was all it said. "Tory."

But that one word was so full of hatred, of disgust, of contempt and loathing, that I recoiled as if I'd been struck in the face.

The mummylike figure kept coming, murmuring my name over and over again as it moved across the porch and then, stiffly, awkwardly, down the wide steps of Nightmare Hall.

It was coming for me.

A strange, strangled sound slipped from between my lips. I began backing up, unable to look away from this strange figure that was heading straight toward me. When it was almost upon me, I finally shook myself free, and turned to run.

But before I'd taken a step, a powerful hand came from behind me and slammed against the side of my head.

My feet came up off the ground and my body flew sideways. When I landed, my right temple slammed into a rock imbedded in the ground, and without a sound, I slipped away from the world, into nothingness.

Chapter 11

The first thing I was aware of was Jessica Vogt's voice saying, "Tory, wake up, wake up!" Jessica lived at Nightmare Hall. I couldn't understand why Jessica, who didn't live in my dorm, was telling me to wake up. If anyone was going to wake me up, it should be Nat, my roommate, shouldn't it?

What was Jessica Vogt doing in my room?

Before that question was answered for me, I realized that her boyfriend, Ian Banion, was with her, because I heard him say, "I checked out her car. It must have overheated." A flashlight played around my head. "The steam must have burned her when she opened the hood. Look at her face."

When I opened my eyes, I saw him standing over me, and Jess kneeling by my side.

Where was I? I peered around in the darkness.

Ian's words sank in as I hauled myself up to lean on my elbows. Overheating? "My car isn't on fire?"

"No. And please don't mention the word fire," Ian cautioned. "After that blaze at the park the other night, that word all by itself makes people nervous. But no, your car wasn't on fire. You thought it was?"

I nodded as Jess helped me to my feet and I saw that we were in front of Nightingale Hall. The lawn and the house and the oak trees and the gravel driveway swam around me like a carousel, making me dizzy.

"Radiator must have a leak," Ian added. "Not a drop of water in it."

"No, that's wrong," I said in a surprisingly firm voice. "I just had them check it at the gas station on Wednesday. I took it to Griff's in town. They said everything was fine."

Ian shrugged. "Well, it's not fine now. I'll put some water in it, but you'd be better off not trying to drive it. Could do more damage. We can take you back to campus. I'll call Griff's for you, and they can come and get it."

"I don't see how they could have missed a

radiator leak," I groused. But at least the car hadn't been on fire.

"Did you fall, Tory?" Jess asked. "This ground is so rocky. You have to be careful."

I couldn't remember how I'd ended up on the ground. But my temple hurt, and I put my hand to it. It came away sticky with blood.

"I think," Jess said, "that Tory should come into the house with us. Mrs. Coates will have something to put on her face, to stop the pain." Peering into my face, she added, "I didn't know radiator steam could do that much damage."

I should have said, It can't. The radiator had some help from the tanning capsule. But I didn't. Because I'd have had to explain, and I didn't feel like it. They'd never understand. I was having trouble myself, trying to remember why we'd gone into that stupid tanning salon in the first place. Oh, yeah, Mindy. To keep Mindy occupied so she wouldn't spill her guts. I couldn't very well tell Jess and Ian that, could I? So I said nothing.

It wasn't until we started up the wide steps to the porch and I saw the wooden swing swaying gently that I remembered the figure in white. It all came back to me in a rush. I jerked backward, my eyes on the swing.

"Tory, what's wrong?" Jess asked when I stopped moving up the steps. "What's the matter?"

"Did you see it?" I asked, my eyes never moving away from that swing. "When you came out, did you see it?" I turned on the steps to point down at the lawn. "There, where I was, was anyone else there when you came out?" I turned around again to look at Jess. "Why did you come outside, anyway?"

"Did we see *what*?" Ian asked.

"We came out because Ian looked out the window and saw your car on the highway," Jess said. "He figured someone might be in trouble."

"Well, did you *see* it?" I repeated, my voice rising unsteadily.

"We can't answer that question," Ian said with remarkable patience, "until you tell us what we are supposed to have seen."

"That . . . that *person*, all wrapped up in bandages. Like . . . like Hoop. Just like Hoop."

"Wrapped in bandages?" Jess looked incredhulous. "Tory, what are you talking about? There wasn't anyone out here but you. At first, we couldn't imagine why you were unconscious, because it didn't look like your car had had an accident. But then we saw your head, and I said you must have tripped and fallen. But there wasn't anyone here with you."

"There *was* someone," I insisted. "It was sitting on the swing, and then it got up and said my name and came at me. Didn't you *see* it? It was right *there!*"

"*It?*" Ian said, puzzled. "Why do you keep saying *it*, if it was a person?"

It was hopeless. Whatever it was that I'd seen, it was gone now, and there was no describing it to anyone who hadn't seen it. "Never mind," I said. "I guess I was dreaming."

Nightmare Hall's housemother, Mrs. Coates, an elderly, sympathetic, gray-haired woman, applied a cool, soothing cream to my face that stopped the pain instantly. And she washed the cut on my head and put some gauze on it. Ian called Griff's to come get my car, and when I had pulled myself together, Ian and Jess insisted on driving me back to campus. Not that I would have argued. I was in no shape to walk back.

But when we got outside, there was another car parked behind mine down on the highway. A big, old station wagon. Someone was climbing out.

"Bay's here," I said unnecessarily as we all glanced down the hill. "He can take me back to school." I decided right then and there that

I wouldn't lie to Bay about where I'd been. I'd just tell him I'd changed my mind about going to bed. I was sick to death of lying.

He came running up the driveway, and when he saw me, he sagged with relief. "Tory! What the hell? I saw your car, and when I checked, it was empty. I thought . . . I don't know what I thought. You okay?"

Judging from the look on his face, he'd been thinking that something pretty horrendous had happened to me.

"Where were you?" I asked when I explained about my car, thanked Jess and Ian for all their help, and Bay and I had begun walking back down the hill. "Have you been to town?"

"Couldn't sleep. Too much on my mind, I guess."

I knew the feeling.

"So, I went for a ride. No place special. Thought about stopping in at the hospital, but I decided that would be pretty stupid. Can't see Hoop anyway, and it might make someone suspicious. For all we know, the police are watching to see who comes to visit him."

That made *his* feelings pretty clear. No way was he going to approve of *my* visit. "Who would it make suspicious?" I said sharply. "Nurse Lovett? She's not an arson investigator, Bay. I think she's more interested in helping Hoop get well than she is in finding out how he got that way. As for the police, I think they have better things to do than hang around a hospital all day and night. And Hoop's parents are too messed up with worry over him to be suspicious. His mother looks terrible."

We were almost to the station wagon. Bay stopped walking and looked at me. "How do you know how Hoop's mother looks?"

I sighed. "I was there. Just a little while ago. I wanted to see if Hoop had talked to anyone yet. He hasn't. Lovett said he can't. She also said he probably won't be able to for quite a while."

"You went to the hospital? Are you crazy?"

Maybe. Seeing tall, threatening figures all wrapped in white coming at you out of the darkness isn't exactly a sign of sanity. "Yes," I said, climbing into the wagon and sliding as far as possible away from him on the front seat, "I am definitely crazy. Or I would have told the truth about the fire from the very beginning. We never meant to start a forest fire, we never meant for anyone to get hurt. It was an accident. Maybe the police would have understood. Maybe they'd just have made us pay a fine, or do community service or something."

Bay started the car and aimed it toward school. He pointed straight ahead of him. "You see that up ahead, Tory? That's the campus tower. See how the lights shine for miles? You told me once that you loved coming back to campus at night because you could see the tower from so far away and it made you feel like you were on your way home."

I remembered saying that. It was true. Salem university felt more like home to me than my own house ever had.

"Even if the police and the state cops had let us off the hook," Bay continued grimly, "the University never would have. We'd be out on our sorry little rear ends. And what other school would take us, with arson on our records?"

"It wasn't arson!" I protested vehemently. How I hated that word! It sounded so . . . deliberate. And what we had done wasn't at all deliberate. It was an accident.

"Tell that to the admissions committee at any school in the country and see how understanding *they* are. Maybe you're willing to toss your whole future away, but if you trash mine with it, I'll . . ." He stopped abruptly and fell silent, his eyes on the road.

I turned my head, very slowly, to stare at him. "You'll what, Bay? What will you do?"

He didn't answer.

"Were you about to threaten me, Bay?" I couldn't believe it. My beloved Bay? *Threatening* me? I knew he felt he had a lot at stake here, but then, didn't we all?

"You know I'd never hurt you," he said quietly.

"Not even to keep your precious political future intact?" I asked bitterly, relieved that we'd arrived on campus. In just seconds, I'd be out of this car and back in the safety of my own room. But what about Nat? Had she awakened and noticed my absence? Where would I tell her I'd been? If I told her the truth, would she be as upset as Bay?

Would she, my roommate and best friend, threaten me, too?

"I wouldn't hurt you for *any* reason," Bay said, stopping his car in front of Devereaux. "I thought you knew that." He sounded hurt now, his anger gone.

"I did know it," I said, getting out of the car, "once upon a time." There didn't seem to be anything else to say, so I just stood and watched as he drove away.

When I got back to my room, Nat was still asleep. She wouldn't need to know that I'd ever gone near the hospital.

The next morning, she wasn't in the room when I forced my eyes open to glance at the clock. It was after ten, late for me. But it was Sunday, and if I wanted, I could stay in bed all day long. I had no plans. I didn't have to get up if I didn't feel like it. Maybe I would just hunker down beneath the covers and hide from the world.

But first, I had to answer a ringing telephone.

It was Griff, at the garage in town. "Ms. Alexander, that you? Griff here."

"I didn't know you guys worked on Sunday," I said, dragging myself upright.

"Why not? Cars break down on Sunday, same as any other day. Listen, Ms. Alexander, you been driving over any rocky roads lately?"

I wasn't quite awake yet. Rocky roads. Sounded like ice cream. "No, I haven't. Haven't been driving much at all, actually. Why?"

"Well, you got a hole in your radiator a good-sized cat could crawl through, and it wasn't there when I checked out your car the other day. Wouldn't want you to think I'd missed something that important."

"A hole? But . . . but I haven't driven the car since I brought it back to campus from your place. And I drove home on the highway, not on some back road with rocks in it. Are you positive the hole couldn't have been there when you worked on the car?"

An offended silence made its way through the telephone line. "There wasn't a hole in the radiator when I saw that car," Griff said stiffly. "This hole here is new, you got my word on that."

But that was impossible. How could the car radiator have picked up a big hole when it was sitting in a parking lot?

And then Griff said, "You ask me, Missy, this hole's been put here deliberate. Looks to me like someone took maybe a claw hammer, maybe a chisel to your radiator, that's what it looks like to me. You know any reason why someone would want to do that?"

Chapter 12

I stood there, next to my unmade bed, the telephone in my hand, my eyes on the window overlooking the Commons. I could see people down there, people leading ordinary lives, doing ordinary things just as they always did on a Sunday morning in the spring. Some were jogging, some walking with tennis rackets in hand, some bicycling along the walkways. Two guys in shorts were tossing a baseball back and forth. Ordinary activities. While here, in my cluttered, sunny dorm room, a mechanic was asking me who might have a reason to deliberately wreck my car radiator. All I needed was to have to start explaining to Griff.

One thing I knew for sure. When you start lying, you'd better be ready to keep it up, because it just snowballs. My snowball was about to get bigger.

"Oh, you know what, Griff?" I said, "I just remembered. I *did* take the car out along the river road. The day after you checked it out. I'd completely forgotten. I was sorry the minute I got on that road, because it was awful, hard and rocky, like a dry creekbed. There were some really huge stones on that road. One of them must have been tossed into my radiator. Can you fix it?"

" 'Course. Cost you, though. Take a few days, too. Don't have what I need here, have to send for it."

I'd been saving for a new CD player. That money would now have to pay for a working radiator. But then, I didn't have much choice, did I?

"Let me know when it's done," I said, and hung up. I went to the window and stood there, looking out. Griff's question rang in my ears. Did I know anyone who might want to sabotage my car?

I added a question of my own. Did I also know someone who might want to lock me into a tanning capsule until my skin was the color of blood?

That depended. Hoop had tons of friends on campus. Had someone figured out that I was at least partially responsible for his tragedy?

And wanted to punish me for it? How could anyone possibly know I'd been there that night?

If I was right, and someone was doing these things deliberately, how could I fight back when I had no idea who it was?

I felt like a fly trapped in a spiderweb, watching the spider with its long, hairy legs ambling confidently toward me.

Just like that horrible, creepy thing that had come at me last night from Nightmare Hall's porch. All wrapped in white, walking like something that had crawled up out of a grave.

It couldn't have been real. I'd been upset, just like in the tanning booth, only more so. Upset about what had happened to the car, and about having to climb that long, dark hill up to that gloomy old house, and upset, especially, about seeing Hoop.

It was probably seeing Hoop that had done it. That, combined with guilt, had sent my imagination into overdrive. If there had really been anything there, Ian and Jess would have seen it when they came outside.

Maybe those tanning rays really *had* done something to my brain.

"What are you staring at?" came Nat's voice, behind me.

I hadn't heard the door open or close. I turned around. She'd brought me coffee, steaming, in a paper cup. I took it and thanked her.

"Nat," I said, going over to sit down on my bed amid the tumble of bedding, "do you think anyone knows we were with Hoop Friday night at the park?"

She sipped her coffee thoughtfully. Then she lifted her head and looked straight at me. "Well, *we* do," she said. "We know it. All five of us. And Hoop, of course."

Now there was a chilling thought.

"Well, I *know* that," I said irritably. "I meant besides us."

She knew about the tanning salon incident, although I was convinced she considered it an accident, but she didn't know about the radiator yet. Could she explain that away as an accident, too? I didn't see how.

Nat stirred her coffee. "No. How could they? Hoop can't talk yet, right? And he's the only one who knows. Tory, Bay told me you went to the hospital last night. That was kind of dumb, wasn't it? That nurse is going to get suspicious if you keep showing up there."

I swallowed a mouthful of hot coffee. "Bay? When did you see Bay?" She'd been asleep when I left the room last night. As far as I knew, she hadn't even been aware that I'd ever gone anywhere.

"At breakfast. Downstairs." Nat's eyes were gray steel as she looked at me. "Tory, you're not itching to tell someone we started that fire, are you? Bay's worried that you feel the need to confess."

"If anyone's going to confess," I said hotly, "it'll be Mindy. She's the real weak link, not me."

"So, when's your car going to be fixed?" was the next thing she asked me.

"Bay told you about that, too?"

She nodded. "Is that why you asked me if anyone else knew we were in the park when the fire started? Because you think someone wrecked your radiator on purpose? That's just ridiculous, Tory. First of all, no one knows except five of your best friends, and second, what would be the point of sabotaging your car? I don't get it."

I felt that hot steam hissing out of the radiator and slapping against my seared skin, and winced. I didn't get it, either, but if making me suffer had been the saboteur's goal, it had worked.

Still, how could he have known I would lean too close to the car when I opened the hood? Most people would have been much more careful.

Of course, if it was someone who knew me really well, they'd know that I don't always think before I act.

"Your face looks terrible," Nat said matter-of-factly. "Does it hurt?"

"No," I lied.

If I had said yes, maybe Nat wouldn't have said what she did, and then we wouldn't have argued. Maybe she would have felt sorry for me and saved it for later. "Tory," she said, a coolness in her voice that I hadn't heard before, "I've worked really hard, practically killed myself to get this far. Becoming a doctor is the most important thing in my life." She gave me a long hard look. "I'm not going to give it all up this early in the game just because you're having an attack of conscience."

"Who said I am?" I said defiantly. Why was everyone getting so nervous about me all of a sudden? It was Mindy we were supposed to be worrying about.

"Bay. You're making him really jittery, Tory. I think you should go find him and tell him to quit worrying. He's not acting like himself at all, and I know it's because he isn't sure about you. He's afraid you're going to fink."

What a rotten thing to say. As if I'd ever turn in my best friends. How could she even think that?

I was so furious, I couldn't say a word. I also hated the fact that she and Bay had been discussing me behind my back.

What was happening to all of us?

I was about to respond heatedly when the phone rang. I snatched it up, grateful for the interruption. Things were bad enough already without Nat and I fighting.

It was Eli. "Are you alone?"

Weird. Why would he ask me that? "No."

"Meet me downstairs in two minutes. I have to talk to you."

I could feel Nat's eyes on me. She probably assumed I was talking to Bay. Something about Eli's voice warned me to let her go on assuming it. "What's wrong?" I asked him, but he wouldn't tell me.

"Just meet me. Lobby. Two minutes. I'll explain then."

All I told Nat when I'd hung up was that I was going out. I knew she thought I was meeting Bay, and I let her think it. Fewer questions that way.

As I hurried to the elevator, I couldn't remember ever having left the room before without telling Nat the truth about where I was going and why. I hadn't told her about the mummy, either. I'd intended to, but then she'd started in on me, and after that Eli had called.

But I knew, as I stepped into the elevator and pressed the lobby button, that even if those things hadn't happened, I wouldn't have told her, just as I hadn't told Bay. I wasn't sure why. I only knew that I would have kept that to myself.

And yet it was the kind of thing you told your best friends, wasn't it? When something scared you half to death, didn't you share that with your best friends, knowing they would understand and be sympathetic? Even if you yourself weren't one hundred percent sure that you had actually seen it?

Why hadn't I told Nat or Bay?

Because something was happening to us, to our little group. I'd thought of us as a rock of friendship, solid and unchangeable, but now I could feel the tiny little cracks developing around the edges.

And as the elevator descended rapidly and the lighted buttons over the door counted off the floors, I had the unshakable feeling that what Eli was going to tell me would only make things worse.

Chapter 13

Eli, in jeans and a gray Salem sweatshirt, was leaning against the lobby wall when I stepped out of the elevator. His glasses had slid down slightly on his nose and his long hair was windblown. He grimaced when he saw my face.

"That burn looks worse this morning," he said, opening the front door to usher me out into the bright sunshine. "You okay?"

"I wish everyone would quit asking me that," I said. "I'm fine. Well, I'm not fine, exactly, but I'll live. Have you heard anything new about Hoop?"

Eli shook his head. His dark, wavy hair slapped against his shoulders. "Not yet. Listen, there's a problem." He sounded worried.

I almost laughed. Of *course* there was a problem. There were several problems, all of them looking, at the moment, insurmountable. "Another one? What is it?"

He glanced around nervously. But no one on the Commons was paying any attention to us. Everyone was busy doing something fun, tossing a ball around, throwing a Frisbee, biking, jogging, running. No one but us was standing on the lawn, stiff as statues, discussing serious problems.

"I've lost my key chain."

This time, I did laugh, bitterly. He'd lost his key chain? Hoop was hovering between life and death in the hospital because of a fire we'd let get away from us, I'd been threatened twice now by a monstrous, mummified creature, and Eli was mourning the loss of a *key chain*?

"No, you don't get it," he said earnestly when I laughed. "I lost it *there*. At the park. Friday night."

I stopped laughing. "Oh, no, Eli, you didn't! That key chain has your name on it." I knew that because I was the one who had bought it for him, at Christmas. It was a thick, clear plastic replica of the campus tower with a hole punched in the very top, where the carillon was, for the key chain to slip through. On the reverse side of the tower, I'd had Eli's name etched into the plastic, because he was constantly losing his keys. That way, if someone found them, they'd know whom to return them to.

But I hadn't once imagined that there would come a time when we absolutely would *not* want those keys found.

"It was plastic, Eli," I pointed out. He looked pale. I guessed that I did, too, in spite of my burn. "It would have melted in the fire, wouldn't it?"

"*If* I lost it where the fire was hot enough. But what if I didn't? What if it slipped out of my pocket somewhere else, maybe in the parking lot? The fire didn't reach that far. The whole thing could still be intact, just waiting for some-one to pick it up and read my name. Even if it did fall out in the fire, the plastic might have melted, but the keys could still be intact. It probably wouldn't be hard for the police to trace the room key."

We *did* have another problem. "What are you going to do?"

"I have to go over there. To the park. I have to look for that key chain. I think if it had been found and turned in already, the police would have been knocking on my door by now. There's still a chance that I can find it. And I don't want any of the others to know. They'll panic if they know I left a calling card back there."

He trusted only me? Any other time, I would have been pleased. Now, it just seemed like one more ten-ton boulder on the back of my neck. "Eli, that whole area of the park is sealed off. No one's allowed in there. The fire is probably still smoldering."

"Tory, you can't seal off something as big as a state park. The entrance may be blocked, but we can go in the back way, by the river road. You have to help me. I can't cover all that ground by myself."

If there was one thing I didn't want to do, it was go back into that park. Not now, not yet. "Why don't you ask Bay? Or Mindy or Nat? Why me?"

Eli sighed impatiently. "Bay is acting really weird, Mindy's been doing nothing but crying her eyes out, and I had a fight with Nat at breakfast this morning. Bay had just told us that you'd gone to the hospital last night, and she made some crack about you turning us all in to the cops. I got mad, because I know you'd never do that, and we had a pretty fierce argument."

He had defended me against Nat? That was nice. Had Bay done the same?

I didn't think so. The impression Nat had given me was that she and Bay were suddenly on the same wavelength.

"Thanks, Eli," I said sincerely. "Okay, I'll help you look. But we're going to have to really look casual when we head for the river road, as if we're going bird-watching or canoeing or something. We don't want anyone to guess that we're headed for the park."

"Maybe I'd better hold your hand," he said lightly. "Then it'll look like we're going for a nice, romantic walk along the riverbank."

I couldn't help laughing, just a little. "Nice try, Eli."

As we walked, I told him about the repulsive "mummy-thing" I'd thought I'd seen. I told him about both times, first at the tanning salon, and then again at Nightmare Hall. I didn't know why I was telling him when I hadn't told Bay or Nat. Maybe because I knew he wouldn't laugh at me, and I also suspected he just might believe me. Eli never discounted things, no matter how bizarre, without considering them carefully first.

I ended by telling him I was sure I'd imagined the whole thing.

He didn't laugh, and he didn't tell me I must have been hallucinating. He took everything I told him very seriously. And he wasn't so sure I'd imagined it.

"You're not the daydreamer type, Tory. Maybe what you saw was real."

I didn't see how it could be. What's more, I didn't *want* it to be real.

But Eli was talking about it as if he were convinced it had been real. "Well, we know it couldn't have been Hoop," he said as we trekked along the river path. "It may have looked like him, but there's no way he could get out of that bed. Sounds like it was someone trying to make you think it was Hoop. But what for?"

"All I know is," I said, "that thing wasn't coming down those steps to shake my hand. It meant to hurt me. If Jess and Ian hadn't come outside just then, I don't think I'd be around to tell you about it now."

"What did Bay say about it?"

"I . . . I haven't told Bay yet."

"No?" Eli looked pleased. "You told me first?"

"Well, I wasn't planning on telling *you*, either. I'd already decided I'd imagined the whole nasty business. It just sort of spilled out of me."

Eli said he didn't see how we could go to the

police just now, and I agreed. And then he said we would just have to keep our eyes open and stick together. I agreed with that, too, and wished it were all five of us sticking together, not just Eli and me. But at least I wasn't completely alone.

"Could have been a joke," Eli said halfheartedly. But I could tell that he didn't believe that at all. He just didn't know what else to say.

Then we were at that part of the path where a side lane veered off into the park. We stopped walking, and hesitated on the edge of the woods, not quite ready to face up to ugly reality.

If it had been summer, with all of the trees fully leafed out, we wouldn't have been able to see any sign of the fire from our spot on the path. The trees along the path hadn't been touched by the heat or flames, and had their branches been covered with leaves, they would have formed a thick, full barrier, protecting our eyes from the devastation.

But it was late March, and although some of the early-blooming trees had new, small leaves or blossoms, most of them were still only in bud and provided a clear view of the blackened acres.

It was horrible. Awful. We stood at the edge

of the forest, Eli and I, staring at the result of our carelessness. I'd seen a picture of Mount Saint Helens once, after the volcano erupted. Nothing but gray ash for miles and miles. The part of the park ravaged by fire looked like that picture. Barren, empty, with only jagged stumps of trees sticking up out of the ground and piles of blackened branches and burned leaves carpeting the ground.

"Oh, Eli," I whispered. "It's terrible!"

"Come on," he said, grabbing my hand and tugging. "We have to find that key chain. While we're standing here feeling guilty, a cop guarding the park could be picking it up and slipping it into a plastic bag as evidence. Hurry up!" Then, when I held back, he turned and said, "Look, Tory, I'm really sorry I have to ask you to do this. It's rotten, I know. I don't want to go in there, either. But I can't do it by myself."

"I'm coming, Eli. I know you'd do the same for me."

That was true. He would have. He'd defended me to Nat, hadn't he? I owed him for that.

We left the river path and entered the woods.

When we reached the burned area, it felt

like we had just stepped into a graveyard. There was nothing left alive where we were standing. I could remember clearly the tall pine trees, the thick bushes, the wildflowers just beginning to bloom. Gone now, all gone. Nothing but blackened stumps, and a thick dusting of water-soaked ash and soot underfoot.

I was so shocked by the devastation that when Eli said, "Tory?" and pointed, it took me a few seconds to realize what he was pointing at.

It was a long, wide white ribbon, trailing along the ground in a curving path, beginning a few yards away from where we were standing, and leading in the opposite direction.

I frowned down at it. What was that nice, clean white ribbon doing in the middle of all that soggy debris? "What's that?" I asked.

Eli shook his head. "Beats me." But he walked over to where the white ribbon began and bent to lift the end of it with one hand. He fingered it for a moment and then lifted his head to look at me with uncomprehending eyes. "It's gauze."

I stayed where I was. "Gauze? You mean, like bandages?"

He nodded. "Yeah. Like bandages."

Every nerve in my body snapped to attention. Gauze? There was a roll of bandage trailing through the burned woods?

"Eli!" My voice echoed hollowly in the empty woods. "Can we please get out of here? *Now?* This is too weird. Eli, there's something wrong. Come on!"

But Eli, inquisitive human being that he was, was already following the white gauze path and urging me to join him.

I didn't know what to do. Every one of my senses warned me that the gauze path meant trouble. But I didn't want to run back through the woods alone, and I didn't want to abandon Eli, either. "Eli, *please!*" I called, glancing around nervously. "*Don't* follow that path!"

But he was already almost out of sight, steadily marching along the curving white gauze trail.

Since my greater terror was of being left there alone, I ran after him, slipping and sliding on the wet ash beneath my feet.

I caught up with him in a small, dark clearing heavy with the smell of smoke and covered with a thick layer of soggy, semiburned twigs and leaves, in the middle of which the white gauze ended. I recognized the spot as being very close to where we'd had our campfire. I did *not* want to be there!

I had just reached out to tug at Eli's sweat-shirt sleeve, determined to make him turn around and go back, when he bent to pick up the trailing end of the gauze.

The minute he touched the ground, it disappeared beneath him. As I watched in horror, Eli tumbled, headfirst, in a shower of wet leaves, twigs and earth, into the hole that had opened up at his touch.

He was so startled, he never made a sound.

But I did. I screamed his name, a sound that echoed eerily in the smoky, soggy woods. Impulsively, as Eli disappeared from sight, I lunged forward, my arms reaching out in a desperate attempt to pull him back to safety.

Too late. I couldn't reach him. He was gone.

I stepped back from the dangerous opening in the ground, my hands flying to my mouth, whispering Eli's name.

And in the next second, although I had heard no sound behind me, heard no rustling of leaves or footsteps on the path, hadn't once had that creepy feeling of being watched, there were suddenly rough hands on my shoulder, pushing, pushing hard.

Crying out, I fought to maintain my footing. If I fell into the hole, who would help Eli get out? I beat the air around me with my fists, hoping to land a blow somewhere on my attacker, but in vain. My feet slipped, slid on the treacherous carpet of wet leaves, and my legs betrayed me.

Screaming in fear, I plunged after Eli into the deep, dark hole.

Chapter 14

I landed on my back on something cool and slippery. It took me a moment to realize what it was. The tarp. The tarp that Nat had folded up and flipped under her head the night of the fire. We'd brought it to sit under in case it rained, although there hadn't been a cloud in the sky.

What was it doing down in this dark, narrow hole?

Beneath the tarp, I could feel that the earth was hard and dry. Water from the fire hoses hadn't penetrated this far beneath the surface. My neck and back hurt from the fall.

Eli was already standing, which told me that he hadn't been seriously injured by his fall. I was so glad that he wasn't unconscious that I forgot I was angry with him for following the gauze trail when I'd begged him not to. I could barely see him. The mouth of the pit was so small that it allowed in very little light from above.

And very little air. This far beneath the surface, the smell of dank earth overpowered the fainter smell of smoke and burned wood. I immediately thought of a grave.

Eli reached down to help me up. "It was the tarp," he said. "It was stretched across this hole and then covered with leaves. Someone set this up on purpose, Tory." He pulled me to my feet. "You could have gotten me out of here. Why weren't you more careful? Now we're both stuck!"

"I didn't *fall* in, Eli," I hissed, standing up. "I was *pushed*. There's someone up there."

He tilted his head, straining to see above him. "Up there? Who is it?"

"I don't know. I didn't see him."

The shaft was so narrow, there was barely enough room for the two of us to stand face-to-face. And I realized quickly that one person couldn't possibly have dug the hole by himself, not quickly, anyway. Eli was six feet two inches tall, and there was probably another six inches of earth above his head. Too deep for one person to dig.

"He couldn't have dug this pit all by himself,"

I whispered to Eli. "Impossible."

"It's not freshly dug," Eli said emphatically. "Must have already been here." He was still struggling to see who, if anyone, was standing above us. "Maybe it's an old well or the entrance to a cave or something. These woods are full of caves."

"Tory," a voice hissed into our pit, "so nice of you to drop by. And you brought a friend with you."

Eli and I fell silent. We stood close together at the bottom of the pit, our heads upraised, listening.

"Can you see anything?" Eli whispered.

"No. Can you?"

He shook his head no.

"This lovely hole you've fallen into," the voice said then, "would make a great barbecue pit, don't you think?"

I gasped, and Eli grabbed my hand.

"Once upon a time, they roasted whole pigs in pits like this one." Soft, evil laughter drifted down from above.

I was speechless with fear. Above us, footsteps slithered softly back and forth in the wet debris from the fire. We couldn't tell what was going on up there.

Then, Eli and I both smelled something at

the same time. I could tell by the way we simultaneously drew in our breath sharply as the odor hit our nostrils.

"Lighter fluid," Eli said softly. "That's lighter fluid."

I refused to think about what that might mean. "But the woods have already burned," I whispered. "There's nothing left up there to set fire to."

"No," Eli whispered back, "but there is down here. *Us.*"

"Oh, Tory," the voice singsonged, "aren't you cold down there? I wouldn't want my guests getting chilled. You could catch pneumonia." The voice changed, became heavier, more ominous. "And *die.*"

There was a pause. "Maybe I can warm you up a little. It's the least I can do for guests who drop in."

I *was* cold now. Icy from head to toe. Still, I craned my neck, straining desperately to see straight up into the mouth of the hole, trying to catch a glimpse of our tormentor.

When I finally did, I wished I hadn't.

Because all I saw was white. Strips of white, wound tightly around a pair of legs striding back and forth above us.

146

"It's *him*," I cried softly, sagging against the wall. "It's that . . . *thing* from last night. All wrapped up like a mummy. Just like Hoop."

"People do still die of pneumonia, you know," the voice droned on, speaking softly, as if he were murmuring to himself. "Everyone thinks they don't, in these days of modern medicine, but that's not true. Burn victims, especially, often die of pneumonia."

"Are you sure?" Eli asked, peering upward. "It's the same thing you saw last night?"

The smell of lighter fluid was stronger now, bringing tears to my eyes. "Yes, I'm sure. Of course I'm sure. Eli, it's . . . he's going to do something terrible, I can feel it!"

"But pneumonia is the least of a burn victim's problems," we heard then. "You know, you don't feel any pain at first. Shock takes over, and you don't even know how terrible the burns are, how layers and layers of your skin have been destroyed, until later when the pain sets in. And I've read that if infection or pneumonia doesn't get you and you do recover, you wish a thousand times that you hadn't. They have to scrub off the dead skin, you know. One of the most agonizing medical procedures ever."

Eli moved away from me, bent down, looked

into the darkness behind us. Suddenly, he disappeared, and I had to bite my lip to keep from screaming. "What are you doing?" I hissed.

"There's something here. An opening."

A sudden surge of hope sent me in the direction of his voice. I had thought the shaft we were trapped in was narrow from top to bottom and that the walls were solidly packed dirt and rock. But at the bottom of the wall behind the spot where Eli and I had stood face-to-face, the space suddenly widened, and it was there that Eli had found the opening. Terribly small and dark, but still . . .

"This must have been an animal burrow," Eli remarked, dropping to his hands and knees to explore the opening. "That could mean there's another entrance. Exit. A way out. I wonder if our friend upstairs knows that?"

We were both peering into the darkness behind the opening when the voice above us called out, "Look out be-loh-ow!" and liquid began dripping into the mouth of the pit.

The smell was unmistakable. It really *was* lighter fluid. Not a lot of it. It wasn't pouring in, or cascading in. Just a steady drip. Still, if we hadn't already moved from our original positions, it would have hit us, landing on our hair and clothes.

The lighter fluid began to pool on the ground in the center of the hole. I moved to cover it with the tarp, but Eli stopped me. "Grab it," he ordered. "We might need it."

I obeyed, darting quickly away from the opening, the tarp in my hands. "He's planning on burning us alive," I whispered in horror into Eli's right ear. "If this opening isn't really a tunnel, if it really doesn't lead anywhere, we're dead." My voice rose. "We'll burn to death, Eli! Or suffocate from the smoke!"

"Matchmaker, matchmaker, light me a match," the voice sang, and we heard the match striking.

"Eli!" I screamed, glancing frantically over my shoulder, expecting to see an explosion of flame behind us.

Not yet. The mummy-figure was still singing away, reluctant to stop terrorizing us just yet. He was enjoying himself. Then the first match must have burned out, because I heard him strike another. Any second now, any instant, the pit would explode in flames.

Eli got down on his hands and knees, told me to do the same, and then said, "Throw that tarp over us. If there's smoke, maybe it'll help."

Then we were crawling forward, the tarp draped over us.

That narrow black tunnel wasn't someplace I wanted to go. I don't like narrow, enclosed spaces, I'm not wild about pitch-blackness, and it occurred to me as I began crawling that there were probably slimy, crawling things in there.

But anything was better than burning alive.

It was impossible to see anything but the outline of Eli's sneaker soles, just ahead of me. The tunnel smelled dank, a little sour, and I wondered if something had died in there. Had something been trapped because there was no way out . . . and died?

The space was so narrow, Eli had to crawl on his belly, pushing through the dirt with his elbows and knees and the toes of his sneakers. I did the same. The tarp scraped along the ceiling of the tunnel, and I had to keep pushing it back into place. It was the only protection we had if the tunnel began filling with smoke.

"Pray!" Eli demanded over his shoulder. "Pray, Tory!"

I knew what he meant. For all we knew, this tunnel led nowhere. When a lit match was finally dropped into that pool of lighter fluid, this narrow passageway would quickly fill up with smoke and we would suffocate.

Still, when the explosion behind us finally came and we heard the sound of flames licking at our heels, we crawled faster, even though we knew that we might well be headed toward a dead end. Literally.

Chapter 15

The tunnel began filling with gray, acrid smoke. As if that weren't bad enough, the passageway quickly grew even narrower. We could barely lift our heads as we pushed with our knees and elbows as fast as we could over the damp earth. It had been hard to breathe before; it was quickly becoming impossible.

My chest and head ached, my knees, hands, and elbows were rubbed raw, and I could feel myself losing hope. We weren't going to get out of this alive. If the passage had begun to widen, if we could have seen a patch of light ahead of us, it wouldn't have seemed so hopeless. But there was nothing ahead of us in the narrow tunnel but darkness.

"Eli," I whispered, slowing down. "Eli, I can't . . ."

"Yes, you *can*!" he barked angrily, and then

got caught up in a coughing spasm. When it had passed, he repeated, "You keep going, Tory, you hear me? You *keep going!*"

I tried. I tried so hard. I didn't want to die. I still had so many things I wanted to do. If I *was* going to die, I didn't want it to be in this damp, dark hole so far beneath the surface of the earth. As if I were already buried.

But I was closer to the smoke than Eli was. The tears pouring down my face now were involuntary and had nothing to do with sadness. They were from the smoke assaulting my eyes. And I simply could not breathe. I tried. But the smoke was gobbling up what little precious air there was.

I didn't call Eli's name again. I knew if I did, he'd turn back to help me, and then we'd both die. Maybe at least he would make it out safely. I felt sad . . . so very, very sad, knowing I would never see anything above-ground again.

When my nose and mouth had filled with the thick, pungent smoke, and there was no way at all for me to take another breath, I just stopped crawling, lay my head down on my arms and closed my eyes.

And the minute I did, the heavy, hurting sadness was replaced. It became instead a fierce, hot anger toward the person who had done this to me. He was probably even now standing up there laughing, believing that Eli and I had burned to death.

No!

From a thousand miles away, I heard Eli calling my name. He said something else, too, but in my half-conscious fog, I couldn't tell what it was.

I don't remember crawling the rest of the way. I don't know how I did it, or how long it took, or how much it hurt. I only remember lying on the ground out in the open, the wonderful, glorious open. I remember opening my eyes and looking up to see blue sky overhead. Then I saw Eli next to me, his glasses gone and tears streaming down his face, maybe from the smoke or maybe not, and I remember him swiping at those tears with one dirty, filthy hand, and I knew he was embarrassed.

And I reached up with my own dirty, filthy hand, to gently wipe from his face a few tears that Eli had missed.

Then we both began coughing our lungs out.

We coughed for a long time.

When the spasms had finally passed, I lifted my head and glanced around. What I saw was nothing but ugly, fire-ravaged woods. But to me, it was the most beautiful sight I'd ever seen.

Eli, thinking maybe that I was looking for our attacker, said hoarsely, "He's gone. I guess he thought, mission accomplished, and split. We're safe, Tory."

For the moment. As grateful as I was to be alive, it would have been stupid and foolish of me to think it was over. It wasn't. Not as long as *he* . . . *it* . . . was out there.

"Isn't it weird," I said, my voice as raw and husky as Eli's, "that the sun is still shining, and it's still Sunday afternoon? I mean, don't you feel like a whole lifetime passed by while we were in there?"

I could tell by the look on his filthy, streaked face that he knew exactly what I meant.

I sat up, painfully aware that every inch of me hurt. My palms, knees, and elbows were bloody and raw, my neck and back hurt, and my chest ached.

Exhausted, I leaned back, against Eli. He felt very safe and comfortable.

Just for that little while, I stopped being afraid of the mummy-thing.

We sat there for a long time, me with my head on Eli's shoulder. We were so grateful to be alive. We didn't talk. We just kept gulping in huge mouthfuls of air that felt wonderful to our aching lungs.

After a long while, Eli finally broached the subject of telling the police what had happened to us.

"We can't go to the police, Eli," I argued in my new smoke-induced croak. "How can we? The first thing they'd want to know is what we were doing out here. No one's supposed to be in the park. We can't very well tell them we were looking for your key chain, can we? And even if we got past that, they'd ask us next what our attacker looked like. Do you really want to tell the police that we fell into a trap set for us by a . . . a mummy?"

"Well, first of all," Eli argued, "it's not a mummy. There's no such thing."

"I just don't think there's any way we can go to the police about today without being questioned about Friday night," I said.

"You're probably right," he finally agreed. "Look, I think we'd better get back to campus. But we can't go back looking like this."

My turn to agree. I didn't have a mirror, but if I looked one-tenth as bad as he did, with soot and dirt coating his skin and hair, I didn't want anyone to see me. It wasn't just vanity. The way we looked would raise a lot of questions.

We were getting up, slowly, painfully, when Eli exclaimed, "I don't believe it!" and began laughing.

I couldn't imagine what he could possibly find funny. But when I looked up, he was holding the key chain in his hand. And he was still laughing.

"Where . . . ?"

"Right there," he said, pointing to a spot covered with fire debris. "I bumped that burned log when I was getting up, and it moved a hair. The key chain was underneath it, untouched."

Then I laughed, too. We had found what we'd come for, after all, in spite of everything. But what a price we'd paid for a key chain that had originally cost less than four dollars.

We made our way back to the river, found a shallow pool at the edge of the riverbank and did the best we could at cleaning up, splashing our faces, arms, and hair with the chilly water.

"It's got something to do with the fire, and Hoop," Eli said as, damp but somewhat cleaner, we walked back to campus along the riverbank. "The way it's all bandaged up like a mummy, the gauze trail . . . all of that is meant to remind us of Hoop. So someone knows we were there Friday night. May even know we started the fire."

"Not necessarily," I said. "If it's a friend of Hoop's, they could just be guessing that we lied about the park and that we were with Hoop all the time. That we somehow got out of the park, and he didn't. And so they're blaming us for that."

"It's like being convicted without a trial," Eli said, "Verdict: guilty."

"Well, we *are*," I couldn't refrain from saying.

That closed us both down, and we didn't talk the rest of the way to campus.

Nat was sitting on her bed when I came in, reading the school newspaper. Her eyes widened when she saw me. "What on earth happened to you? And where have you been? Bay's been calling. So has Mindy. The Sigma Chi thing is tonight, and Mindy's frantic that we're not going to go. She says she needs our support."

I'd forgotten all about that stupid thing at the Sigma Chi house. Mindy was in the running for Sweetheart of Sigma Chi, and her competition was stiff. Two other cheerleaders, and the girl who had been Homecoming Queen in

October, Shannon Wyoming. I'd known about this party for weeks. The thought made me sick. But it meant so much to Mindy, and we had all promised faithfully that we'd be there to support her.

How could we possibly go now? How could we show up at Sigma Chi all dressed up and ready to party after everything that had happened?

I knew I should tell Nat how close to death Eli and I had come that afternoon. She still didn't even know about the mummy-thing. If that thing really was angry about Hoop and the fire, it was angry with all five of us, and it could come after Nat at any time. In fact . . . maybe it already *had* and she was keeping it to herself, just as I was. Lately there was so much distance between us. It was difficult to talk.

I sat down on my bed. "Nat," I asked, cautiously, "you haven't been . . . no one's threatened you or anything lately, have they?"

"*Threatened* me?" She looked so blank that right away I knew I'd been off-base. Maybe it just hadn't had time to get to her yet, it had been so busy with me. And Eli. "What do you mean?"

"Never mind. I just thought maybe some of

Hoop's other friends guessed that we were lying and might have been giving you a hard time."

"Oh. No, no one's even hinted that they know the truth. So far, anyway. Listen, are you going tonight or not? We promised."

"I can't believe they're still giving that party, with one of their own lying near death in a hospital bed."

Nat shrugged. "Life goes on," she said almost callously. "The party's been planned for weeks. Too late to cancel it now. Bay says the thinking is, they all *need* a party at that house, to take some of the gloom away. And I saw Boomer today. He's a Sigma, and he said they felt they owed it to Hoop. That he'd want them to have the party."

Well, that sounded pretty stupid. Still, I decided to go anyway. Because the Sigma Chi guys were, besides us, Hoop's closest friends. And if we were being attacked by someone who was trying to avenge what had happened to Hoop, it could very well be a Sigma member. Being in that house might give Eli and me some idea of who it might be, and we'd be safe enough with a crowd around.

I would have to talk Eli into going. I wasn't sure why it was important that he be there, or why I didn't think of Bay first, but that was how I felt. I wanted Eli there.

"Please!" I begged into the lobby telephone. I didn't want Nat to hear me, so I'd told her I was going downstairs for a cold drink. I'd have to remember to bring one back upstairs with me. "Please, Eli. I need you to be there, too. Anyway, you promised Mindy."

"That was before."

"Before." What a lovely word! If only it were still "before."

He finally gave in. "Bay's going to be really ticked if you and I spend all our time together trying to figure out which Sigma Chi is Most Likely to Be a Killer. You know his temper."

"That's Hoop," I reminded Eli, "not Bay."

Eli laughed. "Haven't had a real argument with Bay yet, have you, Tory?"

"Yes, I have. And he *didn't* lose his temper." Well, not really. Not ranting or raving or throwing or breaking things.

"Well, he has one," Eli cautioned. "I've known him longer than you have. So if you see someone you think seems suspicious, just give me a sign and I'll meet you out on the terrace. And if I were you, I'd make sure Bay didn't see you leave."

Ridiculous. Bay knew Eli and I were friends.

Why would he care if I met Eli on the terrace? I was going to tell Bay everything that had happened, anyway.

Telling Eli I'd see him at the Sigma Chi house, I went upstairs to shower and dress for the party.

Chapter 16

Mindy looked beautiful. She was wearing a strapless red dress that contrasted perfectly with her pale blonde hair, which she had piled high on her head and fastened with a pearled comb.

Nat looked perfect, too, in a black sheath and heels. Me, I couldn't have cared less. It was all I could do to throw on a skirt and sweater.

"You're a cinch to win," Nat said as Mindy climbed into her car. Bay and Eli were meeting us at the Sigma Chi house. "You look fantastic!"

"It's just not going to be the same without Hoop there," Mindy said mournfully from the backseat. "What kind of Sigma Chi Sweetheart shows up at a party without a date?"

I couldn't tell if she was mourning the loss

of Hoop or simply the loss of a date. Deciding I was being too judgmental, I said consolingly, "Everyone knows why you don't have a date, Mindy. Actually, you'd lose more votes if you *did* show up with someone else."

That cheered her up, at least until Nat asked her if she'd called the hospital recently to see how Hoop was.

"He's just the same," Mindy answered. "No change at all. But at least he's still alive. I talked to that Nurse Lovett person. I don't think she likes me." She sounded really hurt at the thought of someone not liking her. That was something that didn't happen to Mindy very often. Maybe never. "She made some nasty crack about me not calling very often. But you know, I don't like to bother them. I know how busy they are in ICU."

"She doesn't have a really terrific bedside manner," Nat agreed. "Still, you found out what you needed to know, right? That Hoop is . . . okay?"

I glanced over at Nat, thinking, "Okay?" I would hardly call Hoop's condition "okay," and I was positive Nurse Lovett wouldn't, either. Maybe Nat was just trying to keep Mindy's spirits up.

Nat turned her attention to me. "You never

told me why you were such a mess when you came back to the room today. We were so busy getting ready. I forgot about it. But you looked awful. Like you'd just climbed up the incinerator. How come?"

I thought fast. I *should* tell Nat and Mindy everything that had happened. We were all in this together, which meant they had a right to know.

The problem was, I didn't *feel* like we were in it together. Mindy was all caught up in this Sweetheart business, and I was still annoyed that Bay and Nat had been discussing me at breakfast. I couldn't get over the fact that they'd thought I might fink on everyone. My telephone conversation with Bay about the party had been brief and curt. He had wanted to know where I'd been all afternoon, and I'd just said, "Out." When he persisted, I'd added, "Down by the river." That was pretty close to the truth. Sort of.

The only person I felt close to at that point was Eli.

Still, Nat and Mindy had a right to know about the mummy-thing. True, it hadn't come near them yet. But it might. If it was angry about Hoop, it wouldn't be targeting only Eli and me. The others had been in the park that night, too. Everyone knew we did practically everything together. Nat and Mindy should be warned.

Right. But *after* the party would be soon enough. I'd let Mindy have this night, and then I'd tell them.

"I was down by the river, and I slipped on the riverbank and fell," I said in answer to Nat's question.

"Did the fire reach that far?"

"No, why?"

"Because you looked all sooty. Not muddy. Sooty. And you smelled of smoke."

"That whole area smells of smoke, Nat. And there was a lot of ash by the riverbank. The wind must have blown it for miles."

As we got out of the car, I said, "Listen, if anyone inside says or does anything weird, tell me, okay?"

They both looked at me. "Weird?" Mindy said.

"Well, I mean . . ." This was impossible. I shouldn't have brought it up since I wasn't ready to tell them the whole story. "I just meant, some of those people inside think we're lying about not being with Hoop the night of the fire. If anyone gets nasty about it, just tell me, okay?"

They shrugged and nodded, but I could tell they didn't understand.

Well, why should they? I didn't understand what was happening myself, and I had a lot more information than they did.

Sigma house was a mob scene, and the noise was deafening. Conversation with Eli was going to be just about impossible.

He was waiting just inside the door. He looked very nice, in slacks and a navy blue blazer, an outfit I'd only seen him wearing once before. Usually, he looked a bit awkward, in baggy jeans and T-shirts. Bay was definitely better-looking than Eli. So why was I so glad to see Eli standing there, and why didn't I notice that Bay was right behind him until several seconds later?

To make up for my screwed-up feelings, I gave Bay a big hug and told him I was glad to see him.

But my eyes, over Bay's shoulder, were on Eli. He caught my gaze and nodded. He hadn't forgotten what we'd talked about earlier, and I knew he'd be keeping his eyes open for anything suspicious.

Bay and I headed into the living room to dance. I felt as if I was walking straight into enemy territory, and judging by the looks we were getting, it wasn't my imagination.

"They don't believe us," I whispered as we began dancing. "They don't believe we weren't with Hoop in the park. Some of them don't, anyway. I can tell by the way they're looking at us. They know we lied."

"They don't *know* we lied," he argued. "They can't know that for sure. They're just guessing. And as long as they're just guessing, we're okay."

I didn't feel okay. I didn't feel the tiniest bit okay.

And although Mindy "sparkled" the way she was expected to, every once in a while I caught a glimpse of her as she danced by me. She was laughing up at the guy she was dancing with, but she wasn't laughing with her eyes. Mindy wasn't okay, either, not really. I wondered what effect the suspicions about us would have on her chances of being picked Sweetheart of Sigma Chi. Everyone liked Mindy. But if some of the Sigmas suspected that we'd been with Hoop the night of the fire and were lying about it, wouldn't they suspect Mindy even more? Hoop sometimes went places without Eli, Nat, Bay, and me. But he *never* went anywhere without Mindy, except maybe out on the basketball court. Even then, she was on the sidelines in her cheerleading uniform.

Mindy was certainly doing her best to stay cheerful. I had to hand it to her. Her only bad moments came when people asked her about Hoop. She got shaky then, and was finally brought to tears by a particularly sympathetic comment from a girl in a white dress.

Bay was being a royal pain, grilling me about where I'd been that afternoon, who I'd been with, and what I'd been doing.

It finally hit me why. He was afraid I might have gone to the police and 'fessed up. I couldn't believe it. What did I have to do, take a blood oath to prove to him and to Nat that I wasn't a fink? Didn't they know me better than that?

"I don't have to tell you where I was this afternoon," I said coldly, pulling out of his arms on the dance floor. "But I'll tell you this much. I did not, at any time today, go near the Twin Falls police station or the campus security office. Satisfied?" And I turned on my heel and stalked off the dance floor.

I went looking for Eli. I found him out on the terrace, standing at the stone railing overlooking a huge back lawn. The air was a little too chilly and windy to suit most people, so he had the covered patio to himself.

"Anything?" I asked, coming up behind him.

"Nope, not a thing." He didn't turn around. "You?"

I shook my head. "There *are* people acting weird," I said, moving up to stand beside him, "but no more than usual. But I've been thinking, Eli."

"Shouldn't do that," he joked. "Dangerous. Could get to be a habit."

I didn't laugh. "Hoop was burned in a fire. Then I was burned in the tanning capsule. Not like Hoop, of course, but still . . . then I was burned by the steam from my car. And then you and I were almost burned to death in that burrow. I don't think for a second that all of that is coincidental. Someone is determined to make us suffer exactly in the same way that Hoop's suffering. To show us what that feels like."

"Or worse," Eli said grimly, nodding. "I agree. The question is, *who?*" He gestured over his shoulder. "Could be anyone in that house. Any friend of Hoop's. Got any ideas?"

"No. I don't know Hoop's other friends that well. Mindy does, though. Maybe I'll sound her out. I haven't asked her so far because I didn't want to tell her what was going on. Not until after the party. If I can't ask her questions without giving anything away, then I'll just have to tell her the whole story now, instead of waiting until later. I hate to do that. I think it's really hard for her, being in this house without Hoop, but I may have no choice. I can't just stand around here waiting for something terrible to happen."

"Where is she?"

"Fixing her makeup."

Eli groaned. "She'll be gone for hours. You know how she is. Maybe you ought to ask Bay instead. He knows a lot of Hoop's friends."

"I don't *want* to ask Bay," I said sharply.

Eli looked at me then. "Don't say something like that and get my hopes up if you're going to go right back in there and make nice with him."

"I'm not." That surprised me. But Bay should have trusted me, no matter what the circumstances were. He should have known, better than anyone else, that I could never rat on my friends, no matter how guilty I felt. He should have known, better than anyone, that if the time came when I couldn't keep our horrible secret another second, I'd have gone to them first, and told them.

I knew I wasn't going to be able to forgive him for thinking otherwise.

So, when Eli pulled me to his chest and bent his head and kissed me, I kissed him back.

And that was something I *didn't* feel guilty about. Not at all.

"I've wanted to do that ever since this afternoon," he said when, smiling, I moved away from him. Then he added quickly, "No, that's a lie. I've wanted to do it ever since I met you, and I've been kicking myself ever since for introducing you to Bay. Dumb move on my part."

Then he reached for me again, but I shook my head. "Eli, I — we — can't start this right now. Not with all the other stuff that's going on. I have to find Mindy, and if she can't help me, then I guess I'll have to talk to Bay."

Eli's thin face clouded. "To Bay?"

"Oh, not to make nice," I amended quickly. "I mean, about Hoop's friends. We have to find out who's after us. So, can we just put *us* on hold for right now?"

"As long as it's temporary," Eli said. "I know you're right. Bad timing, story of my life."

I leaned over and gave him another quick kiss.

Then I went to look for Mindy. I headed straight for the powder room on the first floor. She was probably still in there.

She was.

But she wasn't standing at the sink, applying fresh mascara or lip gloss or adjusting the clip in her hair.

Instead, she was lying on the black-and-white tiled floor on her back, her eyes closed, her mouth slightly open, her long, blonde hair splayed out around her head like a golden cloud. Her legs were bent at an angle, her arms were outstretched above her head, as if she were reaching for something.

And she was lying very, very still.

Chapter 17

I opened my mouth to scream, but the only sound I made was a breathy gasp. I wanted desperately to turn, to run, to get out of there and tell myself I hadn't seen anything out of the ordinary. I wanted Mindy not to be lying on the floor, unconscious. For one tiny moment, I was very, very angry with her for letting this happen. Why hadn't she been more careful?

Because she didn't know she was *supposed* to be, came the answer. Because *you*, Tory, didn't warn her.

I knelt to see if she was breathing. When I was sure that she was, I checked for blood, expecting it to be pooling under her head.

There was no blood. And no visible marks of any kind, except that her lips seemed to be bluish.

I did open my mouth again, and this time a

cry for help came out. Then another, and another. In just seconds, people entered and began milling around, barking out orders: Call a doctor, call an ambulance, get a pillow, give her air, give her air.

I stood up. Mindy had plenty of help now. What I wanted to know was how she'd landed on her back on the floor in the first place.

It only took a second to figure it out. The sink was full of water. She'd been rinsing off the old makeup, planning to apply fresh. And lying in the water, floating innocently, was a small curling iron. Mindy's intention had been to put some new life into her curls.

The curling iron was still plugged in.

I'm not stupid. A sink full of water combined with a small electrical appliance had thrown Mindy Loomis to the cold, tile floor as effectively as a blow to the head.

I knew, even as I stood there looking down into the sink, what everyone else would think. That vanity and stupidity had sent Mindy to the floor.

I knew better. Mindy would never have been that careless.

Someone had *pushed* it in. Someone had slipped into the room, probably tiptoeing, and Mindy wouldn't even have known anyone else was in there with her. I could almost see her, bending from the waist over the sink, her eyes closed, splashing at her old makeup with water scooped into her hands. She wouldn't have heard anything, wouldn't have seen anything. The curling iron would have been at her elbow, plugged in, warming up.

He'd slipped up behind her and pushed the curling iron into the sink while Mindy's hands were in the water.

I was facing the sink now, and I could hear voices behind me saying exactly what I'd anticipated: "How could she have been so careless?" and "Jeez, even my ten-year-old sister knows better than that!" and "Didn't she ever read the warnings on those things?" I felt a pang of sympathy for Mindy.

I wanted to scream at all of them, "It wasn't her fault! She didn't do it! She's not that stupid. Someone *else* did it! Someone horrible — and dangerous."

I looked up to see Eli standing in the doorway. But he wasn't looking at me. His eyes were on the windowsill directly behind me.

I turned around to look.

The window was halfway open, letting in a brisk March breeze.

But that wasn't what Eli was looking at. What Eli was looking at, and what I was looking at now, too, was a small, ragged square of something white.

While Eli watched from the doorway, I walked over to it. Everyone else was busy fussing around Mindy, who was beginning to stir and make little sounds, so no one was watching me but Eli.

I knew what the white was before I even got to the window. A piece of gauze, of course. What else?

I wondered if Mindy had seen the mummy-thing. But she hadn't. As she regained consciousness, she couldn't remember what had happened, and she didn't remember seeing or hearing anything out of the ordinary. That's what she told the ambulance attendants who glanced quickly at the sink, drew their own conclusions, shook their heads, and put her on a stretcher. "I was washing my face," she told them repeatedly, clearly not yet fully alert. "I was just washing my face."

The last thing she said as they carried her out of Sigma Chi was, "I probably won't win now, will I?"

But Hoop's friend Boomer, who was standing beside me, disagreed. "You've already won, Mindy. You're our new Sweetheart. Congratulations."

Pale as the stretcher she was lying on, Mindy managed a small smile.

Pocketing the piece of gauze, I ran after the stretcher to ask one of the attendants if Mindy was going to be all right.

"That curling thing was small," he said as he slammed shut the ambulance doors. "Probably not much of a charge. I think she'll be okay. She's lucky."

Had it been just this afternoon when Eli and I had thought the same thing . . . how lucky we were to be alive? Only this afternoon? It seemed much longer, maybe years ago.

When I turned away from the ambulance, Eli was standing right in front of me. "Let me see it," he said.

I unearthed the piece of gauze and extended it in the palm of my hand. "It got caught on a nail when he was climbing in or out of the window."

"It looks brand-new," Eli said. "It's so clean. If it's the same gauze he had on this afternoon out in the woods, wouldn't it be dirty? Sooty? *We* were."

"We were crawling around in a tunnel, Eli."

"Still, he was in those burned-out woods, standing in the middle of all that soggy ash. How did he keep this gauze so clean?"

"Maybe he changed bandages." I didn't see why Eli was making a big deal out of the little piece of gauze. It told us what we needed to know, didn't it? What we would have suspected, anyway? Clean or not, it was proof that our attacker had chosen Mindy as his target this time.

Bay and Nat, both visibly shaken, approached. I quickly stuffed the square of gauze back into the pocket of my skirt. I knew I had to tell them everything. They would really be disgusted with me now, justifiably pointing out that if I had told Mindy the truth earlier, maybe this wouldn't have happened.

They wanted to follow the ambulance to the hospital. "Okay, but I'm riding with Eli," I said hastily, avoiding Bay's eyes. I didn't want to see the hurt in them. Or anger, maybe, if Eli was right about Bay's temper. But I needed to talk to Eli, and I didn't want Bay and Nat around when I did. Maybe together, Eli and I could figure out the best way to tell the others that someone was out to get all of us.

"Why can't we all go together, in one car?" Nat complained. "I'd rather ride in Eli's car than the Bus. It's nicer." To Bay, she quickly added, "No offense."

But Bay was too mad at me to ride with us. "Suit yourself," he told me stiffly. "See you down there." And he grabbed Nat's elbow and dragged her away.

"So, what are we going to tell them?" I asked Eli.

"The truth? For a change? And I think maybe it's time we discussed going to the police, Tory."

"Nat and Bay will never go along with that."

"Why not? We don't have to admit to being in the woods Friday night. Why can't we just tell them what's been happening since? We aren't even positive there's a connection to the fire, so why would they think that?"

"Oh, Eli, of *course* there's a connection. And I don't see how we can tell the police about the attacks without making them suspicious about the fire. I just don't think that's possible."

Eli sighed as he braked for a red light. "Well, we'll check it out with Bay and Nat. Maybe they'll have some ideas. Right now, I wish I'd never gone near that park Friday night."

I felt exactly the same way.

But that was nothing compared to the way I felt when we got to the hospital and, while

Mindy was still being treated in the emergency room, the four of us went upstairs to check on Hoop's condition.

Nurse Lovett wasn't at her desk. The floor seemed unusually noisy, and a minute later, Lovett came rushing out of one of the rooms, a tray in her hands.

"Oh, dear," she said when she saw us. "What are *you* doing here?"

"We know, we know," Eli said, "we're not family. We just wanted to see how Hoop was, that's all."

She stopped in her tracks. "Oh, heavens," she said in dismay. "Didn't anyone tell you?"

My stomach lurched. Tell us what?

"Tell us what?" Nat said uneasily.

"Oh, I'm so sorry. You should have been told."

"What?" Eli said impatiently. "What's wrong?"

Nurse Lovett looked away, toward her desk, as if she needed to be looking at anything but us. And she said, "I'm afraid your friend has passed away."

Chapter 18

"Passed away?" Eli said. "You mean . . . died? Hoop died?"

Lovett nodded. "Yes, I'm so sorry. But I'm afraid I can't fill you in right now. We're going crazy up here. Three-car smashup. A real mess. They sent two up from ER and another's on the way. I don't know whether I'm coming or going, and neither does anyone else." She bent to rummage through her desk drawers, already having dismissed us.

"Died?" Nat echoed Eli. "Hoop died?"

"I'm sure someone tried to call his girlfriend. Must not have been able to reach her, or I'm sure she would have let you know." She found the papers she'd been seeking and straightened up, moving as if to leave in a rush. Then she must have taken pity on us because she half-turned and, her eyes sympathetic, said, "Perhaps you could think of it as a blessing. Your friend was so severely burned. I've worked with burn patients before, and their suffering is immeasurable. Now, I really have to get back to ICU."

But before she could leave, Nat blew me away by asking hastily, "Did he say anything before he died?" I couldn't believe she was thinking that way. Not now, not when we'd just been told . . . how *could* she? Was she really that afraid of being found out?

Nurse Lovett frowned. "Why, I don't know. I doubt it. I wasn't here when it happened. Just came on duty a few minutes ago. All hell had already broken loose with that car wreck, but when one of the nurses ran by me, she mentioned that we'd lost a patient. When I saw your friend's empty bed a few minutes later, I realized it had to be him. Sure enough, when I checked, all of the paperwork on him was gone. I knew what that meant. I felt really bad. So many people seemed to care about him. But it's been so chaotic here, I haven't had a chance to talk to anyone about his final moments. I'm sure he went peacefully, though. He was heavily sedated."

Then she was gone, rushing off down the hall, her white-soled shoes making only the faintest whispering sound.

We were all transfixed with shock and disbelief. Hoop, dead? Impossible. How could Hoop be dead? *Our* friends didn't *die*. Maybe they got sick, maybe they had accidents and got hurt, maybe they even were burned badly in a fire, but they didn't *die*. Not at eighteen. Except when people were wild and careless. I knew that all too well.

"Dead?" Bay said in a hollow voice. He turned away from the desk, his face ashen. "Hoop's dead?"

"Can we please get out of here?" Nat cried, making a break for the elevator. "I can't stay here another second!"

Like robots, we followed her. We stepped into the elevator when it arrived, and we descended slowly, silently, to the ground floor emergency room where Mindy was being treated for electrical shock.

Mindy. She had no idea that Hoop had died. How were we going to tell her? She'd go crazy.

"If she freaks," Nat said when we reached the emergency waiting room and I asked that question of all of them, "she could say anything. She could scream that it's all our fault. She will,

I know she will. In front of the doctor and the nurses and everyone. They'll ask her what she's talking about, and she'll tell them. And now," she added heavily, "we're not just talking about defying the burning ban and starting a fire. Hoop *died* because of that fire." She fixed her eyes on Eli and me. "You guys are the law students. Doesn't that make us guilty of manslaughter or something?"

I couldn't think. How could I think when I'd just found out that Hoop was dead? But I knew one thing we had to do.

I turned to Eli and said, "The waiting room is empty. If we're going to tell Nat and Bay what's going on, we should do it right now."

And that's what we did.

They didn't believe us, of course, not at first. I wouldn't have believed any of it myself if they'd been the ones telling it to me. But at last it sank in.

"We have to tell Mindy," Eli said. He jumped up and began pacing back and forth in the small, yellow-walled room. "We have to fill her in the minute she gets out of that treatment room. If they decide to keep her overnight, one of us will have to stay with her all night. Keep an eye on her. She'll be here all alone, which puts her at risk more than the rest of us. She's already been attacked once. If he finds out she's alive, he'll come looking for her to finish the job."

We agreed that if necessary, we would take turns sleeping in Mindy's room.

"She's been in there an awfully long time," Nat complained, getting up to join Eli in pacing the white tiles. "Maybe she got more of a jolt than the ambulance attendants thought she did."

Lost in misery, we waited another thirty minutes or so. The waiting room was beginning to fill up with people waiting for word about the car accident. It grew noisier and more crowded. Finally, Bay jumped to his feet and said, "I can't stand this! I'm going to go hunt up a doctor and find out what's taking so damn long."

But just then, a young woman in white came out of the treatment room, a clipboard in her hands. We expected her to head straight for us, but she didn't. She turned and began walking down the hall.

We ran after her.

I caught up with her first. "Are you treating Melinda Loomis?" I asked.

"Well, I was," she said. "Mild electrical shock. She seemed okay when she came in. Her vital signs were good, and she didn't seem to be burned. But I never finished my examination. Are you a friend of hers?"

I nodded. "You didn't finish? Is something wrong? She's been in there so long."

"No, she hasn't," the doctor answered. "She left a few minutes after she got here."

"Left?"

"Yes. I left the room for a few minutes. When I got back, she was gone. I guess she got tired of waiting."

"I don't understand," I said. "She left? Where did she go?"

The doctor smiled. "Well, now, how on earth would I know that? She wasn't a prisoner here, you know. Just a patient. She hadn't even been admitted to the hospital, so she didn't need a doctor to sign her out. I did see the back door closing, though," pointing toward the door in question. "I assumed that was her leaving, because there hadn't been anyone else here. I didn't actually see her, but I saw another patient who I figured was leaving with her."

"Another patient?" Eli said. "What other patient?"

The doctor frowned. "Well, not one of mine, I can tell you. I wouldn't let anyone in that condition leave the hospital. I mean, I couldn't see any actual injuries from this far away, and he must have been ambulatory or his doctor wouldn't have let him leave the hospital. But I couldn't believe that someone so completely bandaged was actually walking out the door."

Chapter 19

When I finally found my voice, I said shakily, "Someone wrapped in bandages left with Mindy?"

"Outpatient, probably," the doctor said matter-of-factly. "Maybe a burn patient. The damaged skin is sometimes wrapped for months while healing takes place." She frowned. "Although that wasn't what it looked like. This bandaging looked whiter, more like ordinary gauze." She shrugged. "Anyway, he seemed to be walking just fine. Is he a friend of yours, too?"

Eli's eyes met mine. A friend? Hardly.

"We have to find her," Eli said minutes later as we stood on the hospital steps. "The doctor said she left before those car-crash victims came in, so she's been gone a while. He could have taken her almost anywhere by now. Maybe back to campus."

"We don't have any idea where we should look for her," I said bitterly," and that's the truth. We have to call the police this time. We *have* to."

They knew I was right. It would be tricky, trying to dance around the reason someone would have kidnapped Mindy from the hospital, trying to explain why we were scared to death, but we had to try.

But first Bay thought we should check the hospital grounds, on foot. "He could be tricking us into thinking he's taken her somewhere else. Won't hurt to check."

The building loomed above us, lights glowing in almost every window, as the staff worked to save lives. But they hadn't been able to save Hoop's. I would think of the hospital from now on as the place where Hoop had died.

No, that wasn't right. Hoop had really died out there in the woods, in the park, in the middle of a roaring inferno. All they'd brought to this hospital in a screaming ambulance was a body, silent and unknowing. Not Hoop.

I couldn't think about that now. We had to find Mindy, before she was gone, too. For good.

We split up into pairs, Eli and I taking one

side of the hospital grounds, Nat and Bay the other, agreeing to meet back at our cars, which were parked near the construction for the hospital's new wing.

There was no sign of Mindy on the hospital grounds. I hadn't really thought there would be. Why would he hang around there, where people would certainly be hunting for her when they discovered she was missing. I wondered if he'd had to hurt her to get her to come with him. It seemed so unfair, that she had survived the electrical shock only to be dragged, probably still groggy and disoriented, out of the hospital and into the dark night. Had she even known what was happening to her?

Probably not.

But she would have if I'd warned her sooner. She would have recognized the bandaged figure immediately for what it was, and screamed for help, saved herself in some way.

We *had* to find her. Before it was too late. If it wasn't already.

We met at the construction site. Bay and Nat were already there, sitting in the front seat of the Bus, but the engine wasn't running. Bay's head was bent over the wheel, the driver's window was open and his arm was resting on the door. "Damn!" I heard him say, and I knew right away that something was wrong with his car. Most of the time, it ran okay for an old car, but every once in a while it got stubborn and refused to budge.

Oh, not *now*! I thought in disgust. There's no time. . . .

"Won't it start?" Eli asked, going over to the door and leaning in Bay's window.

And that was when I saw It. Just a blur of white, really, darting around the corner of a construction trailer off to my right. It caught my eye because it shouldn't have been there. The site was deserted, all the workers had gone home, and there were no other cars parked there.

Keeping my eyes on the trailer, I moved toward it, away from the car. Eli was still talking to Bay and didn't notice that I was no longer beside him.

The white thing moved again. I thought I saw a white leg, a white arm . . .

I don't know why I didn't just stand there and shout Mindy's name. I don't know why I didn't call out to Eli and the others. Maybe I didn't want to scare the figure away. Maybe I wasn't sure of what I was seeing and wanted to check it out first. Whatever the reason, I just kept walking toward the trailer, never taking my eyes off it for fear I'd lose sight of the white thing.

It moved again. In the light shining from the hospital's windows across the street and the walkway lampposts on the grounds, I saw the figure bend, saw a flicker of light . . . a match, a lighter? touching something on the ground. Then the figure straightened up and darted behind a tall stack of bricks.

I'd seen enough to know it was him . . . the one who was so angry with us, who had locked me in that tanning capsule, pushed Eli and I into the burrow, and tried to electrocute Mindy.

It had seen me. It knew we were all there.

So I turned around to shout to Eli and Bay and Nat to come.

And saw the long, long, trail of rags tied together in a dark rope almost invisible against the dirt of the site. It led from the ground near the trailer straight to Bay's car.

The ragged trail was on fire, flames licking along the rope at a breakneck gallop.

I knew then why the figure in white had been bending, touching the ground, I knew what the flicker of light had been. He had been setting the long rope on fire. The smell of lighter fluid reached my nostrils. The rags must have been doused with it before he flicked that lighter.

My eyes moved from the rope stretching across the ground, to Bay's gas tank.

Even from where I stood, some distance from the car, I could see that the rope led directly to the tank, dipped inside and disappeared, a treacherous snake whose poisonous bite would be fatal.

And the flames were racing, racing, straight toward the car where Bay and Nat sat in the front seat, their heads turned away from the gas tank side of the car to face Eli, who was still leaning into the window, talking earnestly. Nat and Bay were blocking his view of the flaming trail.

Fire . . . again . . . another burning. This time, there would be an explosion of rags and gasoline and metal and window glass and headlights and windshield wipers and doors and trunk and hood, all flying into the air in a shower of flames. And bodies . . . mustn't forget the bodies, three of them, charred beyond recognition this time. There could be no hope for any of them.

I opened my mouth to scream, *Get out of the car, get out of the car!* but horror had stolen my voice.

The flames galloped along, swallowing the

rags greedily, a foot, another foot.

Never mind warning them. It was more important to stop the fire.

There was really only one hope. I couldn't stop the flames from devouring the rope of rags, but if I could race ahead of the fire, yank on the section of rags that hadn't yet burned, rip it out of the gas tank, they'd all be safe. The rope would then burn itself out harmlessly on the hard, bare ground.

That was what I meant to do.

And I would have. I might even have made it in time.

If something hadn't come up behind me just then and clamped a thickly bandaged hand over my mouth, an arm around my neck, and begun dragging me backward, away from the deadly rope of flames.

Chapter 20

The thickly bandaged hand over my mouth allowed no sound to escape. I bit down, hard, but got only a mouthful of gauze. And when I kicked out frantically, my feet thumped uselessly against another thick layer of bandage. He might as well have been wearing protective football gear.

I struggled wildly as he began to propel me away from the construction site. I couldn't leave Eli and Bay and Nat there to die! If they didn't see that flaming rope in time . . .

But it was no use. The grip around my neck was ironclad, the hand over my mouth clamped like a vise. I couldn't get away, and although I was screaming in terror, no sound escaped from behind that thick, white hand.

He dragged me across the site and into a construction elevator, nothing more than a metal platform on steel cables, its sides and top open. When he pushed a button, we began ascending. Not far. Two or three floors, I thought, although there were no real floors yet, only steel beams crisscrossing each other to create the frame of a tall, narrow building.

My ears strained for an explosion below us. Please, Eli, I prayed, *please* see that rope in time!

But even if he did, could Nat and Bay jump out of the car in time? And then all three would have to race away from the car to reach a safe enough distance before The Bus was blown to kingdom come.

Was that even possible? I'd seen how fast those flames were gobbling up that rag-rope.

Still, if Eli realized that I wasn't standing near the car and lifted his head to look for me, he'd see the light of the flames. Maybe he could yank the rag free fast enough . . .

The explosion, when it came, rocked our elevator, rocked the entire steel structure surrounding us. It slammed into the night air with the force of a dozen cannons all going off at once. I screamed, began fighting wildly again, clawing, kicking, screaming the whole time, even though my mouth was still thoroughly covered with white gauze.

A giant ball of flame shot up into the sky.

I fought to look down, but even if the grip against my mouth hadn't held my head immobile, we were too far above Bay's car by then to see much.

Beneath the hand that covered my mouth, I screamed and screamed for my lost friends. Using my hands and my feet, I fought wildly to get away, to go to them, but it was hopeless. My attacker was much stronger than I.

Even if I had been able to get free, where would I have gone? Jumping from the elevator at this height, with the hard ground below me, would have meant certain death.

"Don't be so impatient," my attacker whispered in my ear. "You'll join your friends in a second." He pushed my head down, my eyes aiming at the ground. Bay's car was a ball of flame. I couldn't tell if anyone had jumped free. We were too far up.

"See that Dumpster down there?" he whispered, not letting go of my neck.

I saw it then. Another fire, this one set in a huge old Dumpster directly below us.

"They're burning trash," he said. "They do it every night. It's against the law, of course, but no one does anything about it. The crew dumps their trash into the old Dumpster, lights it, and then they leave for the day. Sometimes the fire burns for hours and hours." He gave the back of my head a cruel shove. "You're going to dive into that Dumpster. Like one of those stuntmen you see sometimes in the movies? You'll be burned to a crisp."

He lifted my head and pushed me against the elevator cables on one side. "Now stay there and don't move. I want to show you something before you die."

A siren sounded then. If I couldn't help my friends, others could, and were on their way. The front door to the hospital opened and feet pounded across the parking lot toward what was left of Bay's car. Maybe there was hope. Maybe . . .

But even if Eli had managed to jump free of the car, could Nat and Bay possibly have had time to escape?

I didn't see how.

Was I fighting this battle totally alone now? Was I the only one left from that night in the park? God, that night seemed so long ago! It wasn't. Only two nights ago. But a lifetime ago.

How much of *my* lifetime was left?

The glow from the burning car and the Dumpster below us lit up the rafters. I could see better up here than I'd been able to below.

I clung with both hands to the steel cables, watching as he began taking off his bandages, talking the whole time. "You thought I was punishing you, didn't you? That's what I wanted you to think." First the feet and legs were free, revealing sneakers and jeans. "Your guilt led you to think that. It never occurred to any of you that there might be a different reason." The torso and arms appeared, clothed in a navy blue sweatshirt. Then the chest and shoulders. The figure wasn't as large as it had seemed when wrapped in bulky bandages.

"A different reason?" I asked, clutching the cables. I glanced around wildly, looking for a way out. The only escape was crossing those narrow steel beams, two floors up. Even if I could slip out of the elevator, I'd probably fall to my death. But maybe that would be better than burning to death in that Dumpster.

Unwrapping the neck now. "Yes, a different reason."

The chin, the lips, full and pink, the cheekbones, high and slightly angled, and then, the dead giveaway, the beautiful, clear blue eyes. When she unwound the bandages from the top of her head, her hair wasn't even flat.

The Sweetheart of Sigma Chi looked as beautiful as ever.

Chapter 21

"You have to understand," Mindy said as I stared at her, openmouthed. "At first, I was only worried about you and Eli. I knew Nat and Bay wouldn't talk. So it was you and Eli I had to silence."

"You shut me in that tanning capsule? You were on that porch swing at Nightmare Hall? My radiator, the burrow, that was all you? To *silence* us?"

Mindy smiled at my question. "I decided that whatever I did should look like someone was trying to punish you for what happened to Hoop. A painful sunburn, even if it was a fake one, seemed appropriate. It's funny how your guilt fed right into what I wanted. Even though what happened to Hoop wasn't your fault." Her smile disappeared. "It was mine. I can tell you that now, because you're not going to leave here alive."

I allowed myself a quick look downward. The scene below us was alive with activity. People racing back and forth, some with stretchers, a police car with its blue light whirling on the roof, an ambulance parked a safe distance from the still-burning car, and here came a fire truck, its siren shrieking. I could so easily scream for help. But even if they heard me over the uproar down there, one swift push from Mindy and any help for me would come too late.

"Yours? How was it your fault? We weren't exactly falling over each other to go back and look for Hoop, Mindy."

She shook her head. "I don't mean then. I mean, before that. When we were running from the fire. He wasn't behind me, at first. I was behind *him*. But I was so terrified that my face would be burned, maybe my hair. It wasn't even knowing that I'd never win any beauty pageants. It was the thought of being scarred for life, and knowing that people wouldn't be able to stand looking at me." She touched a hand to one cheek. "I didn't know until then how fast I could run. My mother never let me do sports, she was so afraid I'd get bruised or something. But when I panicked, I put on this sudden burst of speed, and I passed Hoop. Only, the thing was, when I passed him I sort of bumped into him and knocked him sideways. That path was so slippery. If I hadn't pushed him and he hadn't fallen, he would have been able to jump out of the way before that big, tree limb fell down on top of him."

I pictured Hoop trapped beneath that tree limb in the middle of a roaring inferno, while the rest of us raced to safety. I felt sick.

"I *wanted* to stop and help him," she said defensively. "I *wanted* to call the rest of you to come back and help me lift the tree limb. I couldn't have lifted it by myself. But," she spread her hands helplessly, "I could feel that awful heat on my face, like my skin was already burning, and the fire was racing along so fast. I imagined myself with horrible, ugly scars all over my face, and I couldn't stand it. I knew no one would ever want to look at me again. People would turn away from me and they'd shudder. I wouldn't have any friends, and I'd never have a boyfriend again, never win another pageant, never get married and live in a nice house. I wouldn't have any life at all."

You mean like Hoop? I almost said.

"You were going to burn Eli and me alive. That's a lot worse than panicking in the middle of a blazing forest fire and leaving someone who is trapped, Mindy. That's cold-blooded, deliberate murder."

Her cheeks reddened. "Well, I couldn't *help* it, Tory! You were going to tell. Nat said so. Anyway, even though we all agreed, I knew from the beginning that either you or Eli would tell. How could I let that happen? How could I let the whole, horrible truth come out? My life would have been over. And that wouldn't have been fair, because *I* didn't die in that fire. I saved myself." She actually sounded proud. Her eyes narrowed. "You can't blame me, Tory. You should admire me. Everyone thinks I'm so dumb, that I almost wish I could tell them all how clever I've been." She shook her head. "But, of course, I can't. And you can't, either."

I had to keep her talking. "You staged the scene in the bathroom at Sigma house?" I asked. "You were never shocked at all?"

She paused. "Of course not, Tory. That's why I couldn't let the doctor finish her examination. She would have realized I hadn't had any kind of electrical shock. So I split." She grinned. "But I stole half a dozen boxes of gauze on my way out. I was running low. Takes a lot of gauze to completely cover someone my height."

"She saw you leaving. But she thought you were with someone else, someone who was bandaged. So we thought you'd been kidnapped."

She looked smug, pleased with her own cleverness.

"If you were worried about Eli and me," I pressed," why did you set fire to Bay's car? He and Nat wouldn't have told."

"Well, that's what I thought at first," she said, pausing. "But then I decided it would be better to be really safe. You never know about people, do you? If anyone had told me I would abandon Hoop in the middle of a fire, I'd have told them they were crazy, that I would never do something so horrible. But they'd have been right, wouldn't they? So, if I couldn't even be sure what *I'd* do, how could I ever be sure what Nat and Bay might do? It just seemed safer, that's all." She made a move toward me, no expression whatsoever on her beautiful, unscarred face. "I saw that rag-rope trick in a late movie. I was watching it with Hoop. I'll bet he never in a million years thought I was paying that much attention, but I was."

Her face changed then, from something beautiful and as close to perfection as most people ever want to be, into something cold and blank. Looking into that empty, icy mask was worse than confronting a face twisted with fury. You could maybe snap someone out of a rage by slapping them or screaming at them or grabbing hold and shaking them. But Mindy wasn't lost. She knew exactly what she was doing. She no longer cared about anything except saving herself, and was willing to do anything to accomplish that. Even kill.

My back was pressed against the cables. Behind them, I knew, was nothing but empty space and some girders. Nothing to save me if I fell.

I had maybe half a second left to live.

"If Hoop hadn't died all by himself," she said softly, "I'd have had to suffocate him. Because he would have told exactly what happened. I'm so glad I didn't have to kill him. I didn't want to." Speaking like a mechanical robot, with no feeling or emotion, she said, "I didn't want to kill anyone. I had no choice. You can see that, can't you, Tory?"

"No," I said clearly, "I can't."

Her face changed, then. Her mouth twisted in anger as she uttered an oath, her eyes narrowed, and she threw herself at me, her hands reaching for my throat. "You would have *told!*" she screamed, "*all* of you! You would have ruined everything! I've spent my whole life getting people to like me, and they would have hated me when they found out what I'd done. You would have *told!*"

I knew then, as I struggled against those amazingly strong hands, that Mindy was right. We would have told. We would have confessed. Because the lie was so much heavier than the truth, and we couldn't have continued to carry if around with us. It would have dragged us down, and sooner or later, we would have had to unload it.

She knew us better than we did.

We began a wild, frantic dance around that steel platform high above the police and the ambulance and the fire truck and the burning car and the hospital personnel trying to save lives, unaware that I was up there trying desperately to save my own life.

She was so strong. Maybe it was her rage that gave her almost superhuman strength, or her desperation.

But I was desperate, too. I did not want to die.

Directly below us, the fire in the Dumpster

burned steadily. Her hands on my throat, her face a mask of fury, she dragged me closer, closer to the elevator edge. My fingers were still clutching the steel cables, but the skin had broken on my fingertips, they were bleeding, and the pain was intense. I couldn't hold on much longer.

I was sobbing from pain and terror as my feet were dragged closer to the platform edge. Mindy had to bend at the waist to keep her hands around my throat as I slid to a sitting position, still barely clinging to the cables.

Closer to the floor, I saw what she didn't see. As she had unwound the yards of white gauze wrapped around her body, she had carelessly dropped it. It had collected into a high mound of white directly behind her feet. Like a rock. A soft, high, white rock.

She wasn't looking behind her. Every ounce of her attention was focused on me, her eyes, white-hot with rage, narrowed and staring into mine. "Let go of those cables!" she hissed. "Give it up! Let *go!*"

I let go.

She had been pulling, tugging on me with all her might. The sudden release of my grip, like someone suddenly letting go of their end of the rope in a tug-of-war, threw her backward, off balance. She didn't fall, but she stumbled drunkenly, and her hands left my throat.

She would have quickly regained her balance if there hadn't been anything in her way.

But there was.

The heels of her feet collided with the thick mound of gauze, tilting her backward. Her mouth opened in surprise, her eyes widened, and her arms clawed the air for something to clutch.

There was nothing there for her to grab. Nothing but air.

She seemed to go over the edge so slowly, almost as if all those years of ballet lessons had given her grace even when she was falling to her death.

She never made a sound.

It must have been hours, days, years before I could summon up enough courage to crawl close enough to the edge of the platform and look down.

She had missed the blazing Dumpster.

She was lying on the ground right beside it, her arms and legs splayed out around her, her body lifeless.

She hadn't burned to death like Hoop, after all.

But she had landed on that hard-packed ground on her face.

When they turned her over, she wouldn't look anything like the Mindy we had known.

I lay my head down on the cold, steel platform, and cried for all of us.

Epilogue

Since Eli and I were the only ones not hospitalized, we went together to the medical center to visit Nat and Bay. The arson investigators were meeting us there, where we would answer all of their questions truthfully. I had already been assured by the district attorney that I would not be charged with Mindy's death. That thought had terrified me, since there hadn't seemed to be any way to prove that I hadn't pushed her off that elevator to shut her up.

But Mindy had kept a journal. It was supposed to be used to keep a record of her beauty pageant triumphs, but she had used it for daily events. The day they found that journal was the first day in a long time that I'd felt totally free again.

We would have to face the music for starting

that fire. We wouldn't be blamed for Hoop's death, the more serious charge, since Mindy had detailed what had happened in her journal. But there would be consequences, serious ones, and we knew it.

Bay and Nat probably wouldn't have gone along with our decision to confess if they hadn't come so close to death in that explosion. Eli *had* seen the flaming rags, but not in time to yank the rope from the gas tank. The most he'd been able to do was shout at both of them to get the hell out of the car, which they had done. But they'd taken much of the impact of the explosion.

Both of Bay's arms were broken and he had a serious concussion. Nat had been burned on her right leg, broken her collarbone and a wrist, and the entire right side of her face had been severely scraped when she was thrown to the hard ground.

Coming so precariously close to death had changed their minds about confessing, as it had mine. And it drew them closer together, which made me happy, because I want to be with Eli, not Bay. That's okay with Bay now. He has Nat.

We've already talked to the dean. We'll be on probation, possibly for the duration of our education, but at least we're not being thrown off campus. As for the fire itself, the dean seemed to think we might be put to work alongside the rangers, restoring the park. And we'll have to pay our parents back for the hefty fine they've had to cough up on our behalf.

My parents were *not* pleased. "Oh, Tory," my mother said in that voice that means, "Oh, Tory, we thought you'd shaped up."

I hope they'll get over their disappointment.

Mindy's mother never will. I felt really sorry for her. But maybe if she hadn't raised Mindy to think the way she did, Mindy would still be alive. And Hoop, too.

I still wish, sometimes, that things were the way they were before.

But I'm learning to deal with the after.

We all are.

About the Author

"Writing tales of horror makes it hard to convince people that I'm a nice, gentle person," says **Diane Hoh.**

"So what's a nice woman like me doing scaring people?

"Discovering the fearful side of life: what makes the heart pound, the adrenaline flow, the breath catch in the throat. And hoping always that the reader is having a frightfully good time, too."

Diane Hoh grew up in Warren, Pennsylvania. Since then, she has lived in New York, Colorado, and North Carolina, before settling in Austin, Texas. "Reading and writing take up most of my life," says Hoh, "along with family, music, and gardening." Her other horror novels include *Funhouse*, *The Accident*, *The Invitation*, *The Fever*, and *The Train*.

Return to Nightmare Hall . . .
if you dare

The Vampire's Kiss

He had never been so powerful. So strong. So sure of himself. He'd never felt so good.

He stood up dizzily. The world swung around him, the dark and velvet world.

It was nighttime. He'd been asleep for a long, long time.

Maybe he'd slept his life away.

But that was over now.

Something moved in the underbrush. The faintest sound, inaudible to the human ear. But he wasn't cursed with human hearing anymore.

He knew what the sound was, what made it. His eyes glinted in the darkness and he could see the shape of the animal in the deep shadows where it thought itself safe.

Instinctively, he raised one hand and called it forth.

It came, creeping and cowering, repulsive and low.

An enormous rat.

Fearlessly he reached out and gripped its throat in fingers of iron. He raised it up. It hung limply, resignedly in his hands. The only sign of life was the glint of its wicked eyes.

"I could kill you," he told it softly. "I could drink your blood."

The rat twitched. Abruptly he dropped it, already tired of the game. What was the blood of a rat? He wanted more.

"Go," he said wearily and it scurried away.

He heard it then. A human heartbeat nearby. A human was walking down the dark path by the park. A foolish human.

In an instant he had furled his coat around himself, had become a bat and flown up into the darkness. He circled there and saw it. A beautiful human.

A lovely human.

It would give him a few minutes pleasure.

Perhaps, in return, he would let it live . . .

Forever.

NIGHTMARE HALL
where college is a
SCREAM!

THRILLERS

Nobody Scares 'Em Like
R.L. Stine